Snapshot

Snapshot

by

Rob G Lerner

Cover by PJ Hines

Pomanjer Publishing Co., LLC

Copyright

Second edition published 2018
ISBN-13: 978-0999251140
ISBN-10: 0999251147

First edition published 2016
ISBN-13: 978-0692638095 (2016)
ISBN-10: 0692638091 (2016)

Pomanjer Publishing Co., LLC
P.O. Box 986, Vienna VA 22183
Pomanjer Publishing Co., LLC, publishes fiction and non-fiction books that speak to our hearts and catch the idiosyncratic attention of the Pomanjers.

Snapshot

by

Rob G Lerner

Cover by PJ Hines

Lerner's fourth novel, *Snapshot*, is a departure from his previous works and announces his intention to delve deeper into the human psyche. The unnamed narrator of the story is living in the San Francisco Bay area when he meets and falls in love with the strange and passionless Luce. Certain that he cannot live without her, the narrator orchestrates a series of tests to find out if she is capable of loving him. San Francisco, Carmel, and even Lake Tahoe crop up in this bizarre tale, and it is only when everything seems lost that he finds the very thing he has been seeking.

About the author

Rob G. Lerner is the author of four novels, including *Changers* and *Minders*. He is currently writing his fifth, sixth, and seventh novels, while at the same time working diligently to master his pool game, especially his bank shots. Rob is a lifelong fan of Jascha Heifetz and Formula One, and in his free time he lives in Virginia. He can sometimes be reached through the Pomanjer Publishing Co., LLC.

You can find out more about Rob and contact him through:
https://www.amazon.com/author/robglerner

Please leave a review of Rob G. Lerner's books on the Amazon pages for each book. *Snapshot* can be found here:
https://www.amazon.com/Snapshot-Rob-G-Lerner/dp/0692638091

Previously by Rob G. Lerner:

Changers

Book one of the *Changers* series, *Changers* covers the lives of five young friends who discover a secret ability – the ability to turn themselves into animals. It is a wonderful, exhilarating ability, but it also proves to have some unforeseen consequences for the community, the legal system, and ultimately their friendship. (2013)

Minders

Book two of the Changers series, Minders continues the story started in book one. The once solid friendship of the five young people appears irreparably damaged when Luke unexpectedly learns of the whereabouts of the young woman Iowa. Against the advice of his former friends, and in violation of Changer law, he embarks on a journey to find her and rekindle what was once a blossoming relationship. But what begins as a test of his love for Iowa and his loyalty to the Changers quickly evolves into a challenge to his sense of reality and his understanding of truth. (2015)

The Boy Who Loved Dolphins

Timmy is a young boy whose presence is a burden to his parents. His beloved grandfather, his only friend, fires his imagination with wild tales of life beneath the shimmering sea. After his grandfather unexpectedly dies, Timmy and his family vacation at a small, coastal town where Timmy discovers wild dolphins and learns about love, family, and tragedy. (2012)

To Pamela

Chapter 1

The other day I came across a photograph of Luce and me taken some ten years ago in Carmel, California. I had been cleaning my half of the closet at the behest of my dear wife (Maddie can't stand 'clutter,' which means that if I don't immediately deal with something so designated, she will take matters into her own hands and either toss the offending item into the trash or cut it into pieces with a large pair of garden shears she keeps under the bed for some unknown reason) – as I said, I had been cleaning the closet when I pulled down a neat stack of sweaters from the top shelf and noticed an odd rigidity in one of the folds of an old, familiar cardigan. Fishing inside the heavy fabric for the unknown thing, I retrieved a worn and slightly crumpled photograph that had been tucked away for safekeeping and completely forgotten until this moment.

There's certainly nothing special about the picture. It's not a work of art or the last surviving record of a monument or civilization. It's simply a shot of Luce and me standing with our backs to the Pacific Ocean, squinting into the bright afternoon sunlight. You can see that I'm at least a foot taller than she is, and I have to say that my broad shoulders, firm chin, and boyish grin remind me of an oversized, ebullient puppy (this was before I had a moustache). Luce isn't exactly smiling. There is a slight upward curve on her flawless lips, but it looks forced and, if anything, she looks unhappy, especially because her delicate shoulders are angled slightly to one side as if recoiling from something. We are standing at the edge of a cliff, the waters behind us are roiling and seething, and although the sky is bright and blue, there are some dark, thunderous clouds in the distance. As photographs go, it's the kind of thing that gets tossed into the trash every day without the slightest qualm or second thought.

We were lovers at the time. And, yes, the unhappy expression marring Luce's otherwise perfect features is genuine. She was livid for having been "forced" (her word) to pose for the photograph, and she could barely tolerate me for having "conned the old fool" into taking the picture. At the time, Luce's scorn for the gentleman who took the shot was intense, because he had stepped into something "that was none of his business" (again, Luce's words) and touched (carefully, I might add) her precious camera.

That was my beloved Luce. She was always mad about something or somebody, although why it apparently pleased her to be angry about so many things is still a mystery to me.

Chapter 2

I met Luce at a party thrown by a colleague of mine. Tall, well-dressed, with an authoritative bearing and a carefully trimmed, black mustache, he claimed to be celebrating his "liberation" from something or the "beginning" of something else, and, as he handed me a hastily scrawled invitation on a piece of crumpled printer paper, he told me that I was a good friend. In fact, he added, the party was so important to him that he was only inviting a handful of his closest friends. Would I do him the honor of attending? The honor would be all mine, I replied and tried to keep down a rush of sentimentality suddenly coming over me. He smiled, patted me warmly on the shoulder, and left my cubicle. But before he was a couple feet away, he hesitated, glanced over his shoulder, and told me not to be late. If my eyes hadn't been filled with tears, I would have sworn that he winked.

My good friend (I cannot divulge his name, because he is still well-known in our field) and I were financial analysts at an important firm in the heart of San Francisco. He was one of the firm's senior principals (practically a partner), while I was one of its junior employees, practically the lowest person on the totem pole. I had been with the firm for little more than a year when this wonderful invitation came my way, and I have to admit that I viewed the party not only as a way of getting closer to my great friend but also as a means of rising higher in the organization. As it turned out, he had invited nearly a hundred of his closest friends to the party, almost all of them the people I saw on a daily basis. Luce was also one of his closest friends, although she was one of the few there who wasn't an employee (she was in-between positions at the time).

The first time I saw her, she was hovering over a large bowl of punch in my friend's kitchen. I had gone to the kitchen to escape all the people who surrounded me every day (and having the same conversations with the same people I saw on a daily basis wasn't exactly my idea of a wild Friday night), and, as I pushed through the double doors, I spotted this gorgeous woman on the opposite

3

side of the room carefully stirring the contents of a large crystal bowl perched on the kitchen counter under a small window framed by what looked like expensive white silk curtains. She continued stirring the murky, red liquid when the doors banged closed behind me, and every now and then she would bring a ladle to the surface and carefully examine its contents. I was a little surprise that she hadn't noticed my presence, but then the party was quite loud and she was intently focused on the ladle.

Like a naturalist eyeing an unusual specimen, I studied her graceful movements for a few minutes, observing her perfect Grecian profile and the manner in which her thin slacks and blouse accentuated the graceful curves of her back, hips, and breasts, which seemed to float over the bowl as she bent over. But while my eyes were roaming freely over every inch of her, I slowly began to feel guilty for my observations, and I started to fear that my voyeurism might not be appreciated. Not willing to toss aside what might be a unique opportunity to meet this woman, I took one step forward, threw my shoulders back, and tried to come up with a couple of zingers or witticisms that would announce my presence and make my unexpected appearance seem more natural. Loudly clearing my throat, I said as casually and confidently as I could that I was glad someone was finally examining the punch. "Did you find something swimming in your cup, too?" I pretended that I was a natural wit, but when she turned and stared coolly at me, I felt stupid and immediately regretted trying to be someone or something I wasn't. When she realized that she didn't know me, she grumbled something and returned to the bowl.

Despite this setback, I was still determined to meet her, and so I walked over to the bowl, grabbed a small crystal cup from a nearby stack, and prepared to drink as much punch as it took to achieve my goal. But just as I was about to dip the edge of my cup into the blood-red liquid, she checked my hand with hers and shook her head. The slight touch of her cool, moist fingers sent a shiver through my body and I retracted the cup and unconsciously took a step back. When she

4

didn't look up, I asked her if something was actually wrong with the punch and added that I would be happy to help if she needed it. It's interesting how lame, uninspired statements can sometimes get better results than cool, offhanded quips. Poking her slim index finger into contents of the ladle and swirling it around, she explained without looking up that she was trying to recover a watch that had slipped off her wrist and taken a nosedive into the bowl while she was filling a glass.

She reddened becomingly after admitting this and then told me that her name was Luce, noting that she had been named after someone in her family. I responded with my name and mentioned that I didn't know of anyone in my family with a similar name. She smiled briefly and turned back to the bowl and ladle, explaining as she continued fishing for the watch that it had been a gift and that it was extremely valuable. She added that it had slipped off her wrist because the clasp was broken and wouldn't stay closed. I nodded sympathetically, although I was somewhat surprised that anyone would risk losing such a watch by wearing it with a broken clasp. A few minutes later, she managed to snag it and coax it slowly to the surface. When securely in hand, she wiped it off on one of the white curtains and examined it carefully, after which she slipped it back on and snapped it securely in place. The watch was one of those famous Swiss brands, and after observing it on her arm for a few moments, she turned to me and smiled as if to suggest that the accidental dunk was just one of those things. I couldn't help wondering if she had purposely dropped it into the bowl.

I tried to appear knowledgeable and understanding, smiling as if such things happen to everyone from time to time. I even nodded sympathetically when she told me about someone who lost a gold ring while baking a cake for a sick friend. The ring, which like the watch was extremely valuable, turned up a few days later when the sick friend broke her front tooth on it while eating a piece of the cake. Luce paused for a moment and then started laughing. As it turned out, the sick friend was a high-powered attorney who would have sued the solicitous friend had she been certain that the case wouldn't rupture their relationship. Well, this lame story led to other tales about her friends, her neighbors, and people in the news, which meandered into a long conversation between us about virtually everything under the sun from attorneys to gold jewelry, and from gold jewelry to gold filings and dentists, watches, valuable items in general, less-than-valuable items in particular, perfume, body odor, music, movies, and photography. It turned out that Luce was keenly interested in photography, particularly nature photography, and she mentioned that she knew one of the greatest photographers who had ever lived, a "genius" who specialized in oversized images of insects eating their mates (I don't recall the name of this sadist). However, our conversation didn't end in the kitchen, but continued its meanderings and contortions into the living room, where we sat on a couch on the corner and joked about some of the people at the party. Two hours later, I drove her to her apartment because she didn't have a ride, and within three months we were practically inseparable.

Chapter 3

Luce – her real name was Lucinda, but no one called her that, and no one to my knowledge ever called her Lucida, Lucy, Cindy, or even Lu, all of which would have elicited a snarl and some well-chosen words in response – Luce (pronounced "loose") was in her mid-thirties when we met. She was five years older than me, but she looked much younger than her years, perhaps in her late twenties. In fact, she often claimed to be in her early twenties, which I had no reason to doubt until I saw her driver's license. I had been rummaging through her purse one evening while she was in the bathroom when I found it in one of the side pockets, wrapped in a tissue. I was a little taken aback that she was nearly thirty-six, but as I thought it over I realized that it didn't matter because she was beautiful, and I was confident that she would keep her looks well into middle age. Petite and perfectly proportioned, Luce had blond hair (probably dyed) which she wore in a pageboy, dark-blue eyes that often appeared black, and flawless skin that was unaffected by her frequent frowns and scowls.

Luce's personality was every bit as distinctive as her looks. While generally charming and engaging, she could be temperamental, capricious, and acerbic when something didn't go her way or when the mood suited her. This naturally made our relationship a challenge sometimes, although it also made her personality a little intriguing. One time, early in our relationship, I described my job at the firm, explaining how important people and large corporations made decisions on the basis of what I said, and as an example I told her about a client who altered the financial-reporting structure of his million dollar empire because of the advice I had given him. I may have stretched a point or two for effect, but my story was essentially honest and accurate – and not once during the telling did I get the sense that she doubted anything or failed to understand the importance of what I did. When I was finished, Luce smiled vaguely and then turned away and stared silently out the window. We were in my living room at the time, and the large window behind her offered a lovely view of the city and a corner of a nearby park. But as she turned away, I could have sworn that she called me a liar under her breath, even though there was nothing in her demeanor to suggest that she didn't believe me or had caught onto certain embellishments. Out of curiosity, I asked her if she had any questions either about my work or my client. She shook her head and mumbled something about needing to think for a few minutes.

I don't remember what was said immediately after this, but I distinctly recall how she peppered our conversations throughout remainder of the day with offhanded remarks and interpolations which suggested that she hadn't entirely accepted my account. "Is this another one of your stories?" she asked at one point, and "Do you ever listen to yourself?" she queried at another. One time, she shook her head and demanded, "Do you think I'm an idiot?" And after each comment, she smiled innocently as if she were joking or playing a silly game. Did she really think that I was telling tall tales or exaggerating my claims? If she did, then I don't know why she didn't call me out directly, since she was never shy about expressing her thoughts, even if she bruised feelings or elicited anger. But that was Luce in a nutshell – it was difficult to tell how she would react to something, and it was almost impossible to be certain about her ultimate intentions. One moment she would smile becomingly, caress me with her dark, liquid eyes, and the next accuse me of the most outrageous things. Given enough time, I have little doubt that she could drive someone like me insane, but I couldn't have dropped her even if my life depended on it.

Do you still remember where the picture was taken? Luce and I had been together for nearly six months when I got the bright idea to take her to Carmel for the week (I had enough vacation time and, as far as I could tell, she could come and go as she pleased). Maybe such a trip sounds a little premature – after all, we were in many ways still getting to know one another – but at the time it sounded like exactly the right thing to take our relationship to the next level, as it were. We were having a great time together, and since we weren't exactly kids, we had the maturity to deal with just about anything that could come our way. So, why not? The idea came to me one afternoon at the hairdresser's. While I was resting comfortably in the chair, I began thumbing through a style magazine and came across an advertisement for a bed and breakfast in Carmel. There wasn't a picture of the Hacienda Plantation in it, but there plenty of images of the surrounding area and a detailed description beneath that was arranged like a sonnet and filled with such poetic words as "getaway" and "romantic" and "renewal" and "take it to the next level" (the latter, however, might be a product of my imagination). It came to me that this was the very thing we needed (a place away from the city and the people we knew) when the stylist held a mirror to the back of my head and exposed the barren spot. Yes, at the time it made sense, and I was positive that if Luce agreed, it made sense to her, too.

Apparently, it did, for she eagerly accepted my proposal with an unemotional "sure," and then turned the conversation to matters in which she was the heroine and principal actress (mainly past relationships, current friends, and future fights with her building management if something wasn't fixed). My confidence might have been greater had we talked about it for a few minutes, but when she launched into an assessment of her building manager, who, according to her, was a fool and smelled like cheese, I began to entertain some minor doubts about the advisability of taking the trip at this time. Even though we were practically living together, we had never ventured beyond the narrow confines of the city and my apartment, and so there was every reason to be concerned that we might come through the trip in a way that neither of us could have foreseen. I realize now that I should have pressed the issue, but when she started in on some other "idiot," it occurred to me that her laconic "sure" could only mean one of two things – either she wasn't worried and thus had complete confidence in us, or else she possessed an inner safety net of some kind that protected her from catastrophic, emotional falls – and as a result my concerns evaporated and I looked forward to the big day and week.

9

Early one Saturday morning a couple weeks after this, we set out for Carmel. I couldn't have imagined a morning less promising or more at odds with our general mood than this one. The air was cool and breezy, and dark, foreboding clouds filled the sky well beyond the city. Still, we didn't let any of this dampen our enthusiasm – and, yes, Luce now seemed excited by the trip – because we were together and leaving the distractions of the city behind us. In fact, at one point along the way, Luce, for the first and only time since I've known her, began to sing along with some of the inane songs that were blasting through the radio. She truly had a wonderful voice, and, even though she had trouble keeping time with the music, it was enough to make me feel warm inside and wish that the trip would never end.

At Luce's insistence, we took the longer and more scenic route on the Pacific Coast Highway, and by the time we were past Half Moon Bay, everything suddenly changed – the air was warm, clouds were gone, and the sky was clear and bright. The fields on either side of the road were green and shimmered in the sunlight, and the ocean...I don't recall ever having seen the Pacific Ocean so beautiful. Its color ranged from a sparking cobalt blue near the shore to a mellow ultramarine farther out where it merged with the equally intensely colored sky. We made a quick stop a little past Santa Cruz to stare at the ocean, and another a few miles farther on to feel the warm, ocean air and to get a quick bite to eat. While we made a couple of additional stops to do something or other, each one served to increase my desire to get to Carmel and our hotel, for by the time we made our last stop, I was convinced that the only way we could be truly alone and free to experience this next phase in our relationship was to be connected to the hotel – and to be so connected was to be (metaphorically, at least) disconnected to our lives in the city.

I thought Luce felt the same way – after all, when she wasn't singing or rattling on about one thing or another, she practically said as much with her appreciation of the sights and sounds along the way. And yet the second we reached the outskirts of Carmel and were only a few minutes from our hotel, she refused to go any farther, not even to drop off the luggage, which filled the car's trunk and most of its back seat, and demanded that we first take the famed 17-mile Drive. And after that, she added, she wanted to see some of the town and have dinner "at a nice place, for a change." I tried to protest (pleasantly, of course) but Luce would have nothing of it, informing me that since I was the driver, she had the "right" to choose where I was taking her. "Besides," she continued, "we've done everything you wanted to do and not a single thing I wanted to do." I refused to argue with her and, instead of driving into the hotel parking lot, which was now practically across the street, I turned the car back onto Ocean Drive, and headed toward the intersection that would take us to the 17 Mile drive.

I admit that I was a little impatient with Luce's capriciousness (and who wouldn't be?), since it reflected her lack of concern for my wishes and feelings. Equally important, I was concerned that by postponing our connection to the hotel, we were still retaining the ties that bound us to the Bay Area and our lives there, which this trip was supposed to eliminate, at least for a short time. But it simply wasn't true that everything we did between San Francisco and Carmel was at my insistence and contrary to her wishes. We both agreed (explicitly or otherwise) to stop along the road to appreciate the scenery, we both agreed to have lunch at the foul-smelling seafood shack outside Santa Cruz, and we both agreed to I don't know what else. Yes, I insisted that we stop at the fruit stand, because I needed a bathroom break and because I wanted some artichokes for later in the evening. But we took her route to Carmel, we listened to her music on the radio, and we drove at the rate of speed that she deemed appropriate (she kept insisting that I was driving too fast). However, my impatience, if you can call it that, was mollified shortly after we passed the ranger's station and started on the 17 Mile Drive, for we immediately entered a dark wind-swept forest that gave off a scent which, mingled with the salty ocean air, was nothing less than intoxicating.

Chapter 4

The guidebooks tell you that the 17 Mile drive is a long and winding road that runs from Carmel to the hills and back, and that along the way it offers fabulous vistas of Monterey Bay and the Santa Cruz Mountains, as well as some weather-beaten evergreen forests, the Lone Cypress (the famed cypress tree that appears to be growing out of a large boulder overlooking Monterey Bay), Pebble Beach golf course, and some of the most expensive homes you'll find anywhere.

On the whole, the guidebooks are correct, and practically every inch of the drive, from beginning to end, offers some delight that cries out either for a closer inspection or a moment of dumb amazement. I don't know how long it takes to traverse the entire seventeen miles, or even if the route is seventeen miles long, because it's difficult to drive the entire length without stopping several times to admire the scenery and inhale the cool ocean air. With a good chunk of the day still ahead of us, we were no longer in a rush (I conceded that the hotel could wait) and so, like so many others who had gone before us, we took our time and savored the experience, sometimes stopping to examine the gnarled foliage, sometimes pausing to soak in an ocean view, watching the roiling white waves crash against the huge, seagull-speckled rocks that line parts of the shore. Oh, it was even more beautiful as the sun began edging toward the horizon, filling the sky with warm light and golden clouds, and Luce – well, Luce was so beautiful, so pleasant, so engaging that it was hard to believe this wasn't some amazing dream.

Interestingly, Luce told me on our way to Carmel that she intended to collect a small rock or twig from every place we stopped as a memento of our journey. She pulled out a marker from her purse to show me what she would use to inscribe the time, day, and year on each treasured object. For a while, I also thought that she intended to record our presence in Carmel in a similar fashion using an expensive German camera that she had acquired a few days before the trip. She wouldn't give me a lot of details about the acquisition, but it was obvious that it had set her back several thousand dollars – and since she could have made a respectable record of our trip with just about any camera, it was equally obvious that she had made this investment with another investment in mind, that is, in our relationship. I couldn't help smiling warmly the first couple of times I watched her carefully extract the camera from its handcrafted leather case, especially when she cradled it closely to her heart. Shortly after this, my smiles faded because she never used the treasured object. Time after time, she would extract it from the case, tinker with its knobs and dials, check the viewfinder for proper functioning, and then gently slide the camera back into its case without once having engaged its shutter. It was an extraordinary object, all right, but she acted as if its purpose lay in its appearance, weight, and knobs, not in its ability to record the moments we shared on our journey. Okay, so maybe I'm stressing the camera's lack of use too much, since she might have taken hundreds if not thousands of pictures had our trip not been severely truncated. But one thing I can't stress too much – that bloody camera was at the root of our problems and nearly ended our relationship.

Well, I suppose the camera wasn't the sole cause of our problems that day. We had a lot of issues that were completely unrelated to the camera, but all of them together were nowhere near as divisive as the one involving the camera. Early on, for example, when we were just outside of Half Moon Bay, we argued briefly about whether to keep the car widows up or down. I wanted to breathe the invigorating salt air, while Luce insisted that it was too cold to open the windows. "Besides," she added, "salt air stinks." We compromised by keeping the windows closed until Watsonville, where it was warmer and where we got into a brief but heated exchange at the fruit stand over the time she had to wait while I visited the facilities. When this spat seemed over, I apparently caused another row when I picked out a few artichokes. Because I didn't have anything smaller than a twenty – which the checker, a heavyset older woman with a sneer on her face, refused because, she said, if she cashed it, then she would have to do the same for everyone else – I turned to Luce and asked her pleasantly if she would pay. Luce, however,

13

folded her arms and refused, explaining in front of the sneering checker that since I was the "one who wanted the nasty things," I should be the one who paid. (It occurred to me then that since I was the one who suggested our trip, I was going to be the one shelling out for everything.) There were a few other incidents along the way, but none of them could match the sheer bitterness surrounding the first photographs taken with her precious camera.

By the time this erupted, we had moved beyond the earlier incidents and were getting along quite acceptably. We had been driving for about ten minutes along one particular stretch of the 17 Mile Drive when I noticed a section of the coast that seemed particularly inviting. Spotting a narrow clearing off the road, I darted into it and brought the car to a halt. Naturally, Luce wasn't pleased because I hadn't consulted her about stopping, but once we got out of the car and stretched our legs, she appeared willing to let the matter drop as long as I didn't try to pull anything like it again. A few feet from the car, we found a narrow trail that disappeared into a stand of trees and appeared to meander toward the ocean, which completely dominated the horizon save for a few patches of trees and large rocks. It took no more than ten minutes or so to reach the place that figured into the photograph, which was at the edge of a series of narrow, shallow cliffs that offered spectacular views of blue water and island-like boulders that were the home to seagulls, seals, and thousands of other creatures. There was one spot a few feet away that looked particularly inviting, and so we stopped there to take in everything – the edge of the cliff, the rock-like islands, and, for me, the smell of the ocean as it permeated the air surrounding us.

Standing a few feet from the edge, we could see the green waves of the ocean exploding relentlessly against the cliff face, sending hazy white mists upwards that on wilder days must have reached the top. The sky was filled with wispy, white clouds, and a mild, cool breeze was whipping around our faces and feet. Perhaps a hundred yards out over the water, dozens of seagulls were hovering over something below the surface, screeching either to themselves or to something in the water. Oddly enough, the plaintive cries of these birds, which I could only catch intermittently, intensified my feelings for Luce (they seemed to be expressing something inside me); and, as I looked across the limitless horizon, it wasn't hard to believe that we were the only people on earth and were standing together at the edge of eternity. I know this will sound silly and sentimental, and maybe even strange given our bickering on the road, but at the moment this was how I felt and my legs were shaking slightly because of it. Turning toward her, looking deeply into her dark eyes, I was about to say something touching and sentimental when she announced that she was going to take a picture.

"It makes sense, I guess," she added, justifying her intention.

Her tone of voice took me by surprise. It was cold and emotionless, and completely at odds with the warmth and passion that filled my heart. In fact, if I hadn't known better, I would have thought that she was bored and that the mindless act of taking a picture was only thing at the moment that could alleviate the emptiness inside her. But since I did know better, and I was hopeful that I understood the working of her heart, I was practically certain that the flat sound to her voice was due to the sound of the waves (it sometimes was difficult to hear her) and to the thick, salt-filled air, which even distorted the strident screeches of the now-irritating seagulls floating directly overhead. I remember watching her after this, observing her careful movements while she bent over the camera and extracted it from the case using her thumb and forefinger. I didn't detect anything particularly unusual about this, not even her silence as she prepared the camera for its maiden use.

When she balanced the camera in the palm of one hand and began fidgeting with the dials using the fingers of the other, it occurred to me that she was going to take a picture of us and memorialize a moment when we were alone and intimate with one another. Standing in this garden of delight, waiting for the picture that would seal our image as a couple to us and everyone else who saw the picture, I felt a rush of emotion come over me and for a few seconds I wanted to get down on my knees and tell her everything that was in my heart. I didn't, of course, it was a little premature, but while I waited for her to cease all the superfluous and irritating movements (she was adjusting and readjusting the same dials again and again) and take the picture, I began to imagine all sorts of pictures that we could take after the first, each one showcasing our intimacy to anyone who chanced upon the pictures. In one, we were standing shoulder to shoulder, our arms around each other's waist. In another, I was seated on the rock while Luce rested comfortably on my lap, her soft, bare arms draped around my neck. 'Who knows?' I said to myself, "Luce might have something better in mind, perhaps a picture of us kissing.'

As it turned out, Luce did have something better in mind, at least to her mind: She informed me that she was going to take a picture of the small patch of ivy at the base of the rock and that we could leave after that.

Chapter 5

The tone of her voice was slightly different this time. It was still infused with boredom, but now it also sounded a little preemptory, as if she were lecturing a little tour group whose incessant questions about everything were getting on her nerves. But since I'm an optimist, I was still confident that after taking the picture of the ivy, she would pause and listen to the waves crashing against the cliffs, feel the mist from the water as it swirled around us, and catch sight of the seagulls floating gracefully overhead – she would notice all this and, her heart suddenly swelling, turn to me and demand an image of us for all eternity. Unwilling to leave things to chance, I suggested that after taking a picture of the ivy, she might like to take one of us, maybe sitting beside the plant or, better still, standing with our backs to the ocean.

"To be honest," I added pleasantly, "the greenest ivy pales in comparison to your beauty."

Luce shot me an icy glance and then began tinkering with the camera again, this time angrily as if my statement had caused the camera to malfunction. After a few moments of apparently futile tinkering (during which I was hesitant to proffer any help, since she didn't look like she wanted any advice), she mumbled something that got lost in the wind, or at least most of it. It sounded like she said that taking the picture I suggested would be a waste of time. (Of course, she might have said that taking a picture of "plus would be a complist wist of fly slime." If this were the case, I was certain that she wasn't interested in explaining what a "complist wist" was or whether "fly slime" was dangerous or not.) Still, there was no mistaking the languid arch of her shoulders or the shake of her pretty head, which was part and parcel of whatever it was that she actually said. There was also no mistaking the fact that as soon as she finished re-readjusting the dials and levers, rectifying whatever I had verbally misaligned, she turned her back to me and, squatting down opposite the ivy, positioned herself to take a perfect picture. I

17

let it pass, I let it all pass, because I was fairly certain that once she got her precious image, we could settle down to the business of getting a nicer one of ourselves.

I was mistaken. No sooner had she taken a shot of that wretched plant than she began easing her precious contrivance back into its leather case, at the same time turning and walking away from the area. Hoping that she had simply forgotten my request, I asked her to wait a second to get a picture of us with our backs to the ocean. "Isn't a beautiful view?" I said, holding my arm out and motioning toward the water.

"Oh, some other time," she replied and tucked the camera and case under her arm as if she had no intention of exposing the camera to such a frivolous use.

"Why not? Come on, it'll be fun," I said, and innocently reached for the camera case. My intentions were completely honorable, and I would never have tried under any circumstances to take the camera from her. I was simply reaching for it the way she might have reached for the car keys to retrieve something from the trunk, or the manner in which she might have grabbed my napkin to dab something off my cheek. But Luce didn't see it that way. When I reached for the camera, she jerked it violently away as if I were trying to steal it and, like a child, held it behind her back.

"Leave it alone! It's not your camera," she growled with a childish petulance that shocked me.

"What?" I replied in a feeble, somewhat embarrassed tone, not quite believing my eyes or ears. 'Is she joking?' I asked myself.

"I took a picture, and I'm not going to take another one." She paused and stared at my shocked face (I suspect that my jaw was at least partly open in surprise). "And stop pressuring me to use my camera. Get your own."

"I'm sorry," I finally stammered out. "I'm sorry. I'm not trying to pressure you into doing anything. I…I just thought a nice picture of us in front of the water would be…nice."

"Well, don't grab for the camera," she said quietly, now holding the camera at her side with the strap wound tightly around her wrist and forearm. Seconds later, when her features began to soften, I thought the worst was over and the loving individual I once knew had come back. I was mistaken, for when I took a step closer to her (I only wanted to touch her in a tender, forgiving way), she tightened her grip on the camera and made a slight backward movement as if to tuck it under her armpit, should it become necessary.

We stood quietly for several moments at the little intersection of the trail. Neither one of us was willing to make the first move, and while we pretended to appreciate the water or the screeching birds overhead, we actually watched each other out of the corner of our eyes. Uncomfortable with this strange subterfuge, I decided to test the waters once again to see if she had really calmed down.

"Are you mad at me," I asked, "because I reached for your camera? I was kidding and didn't mean anything by it."

"Who's mad? Let's just forget it. Have you seen enough here?"

"No, really, are you upset about something?"

"No, I'm not upset about anything. I'm not upset about the camera either."

"You acted like it."

"It's your imagination."

"Okay, I guess I jumped to a conclusion. You did sound mad, though."

"I'm not." And having said this, she leaned over and gave me a brief, cold peck on the cheek.

Okay, so what was I supposed to think? It was obvious that she got mad about the camera, and it was equally obvious that she was still mad with me. I could tell, because there was something in her peck that didn't feel right, something that felt forced and that seemed meant to appease me. Furthermore, she still didn't hand over the camera, which of course could have been an oversight. But since I was willing write off this incident as being little more than a silly miscommunication, I decided to raise the portrait idea again.

"I believe you. I just wanted to make sure everything's okay." I tried to smile warmly. "So what do you think about a picture of you and me with our backs to the water?"

Luce frowned angrily, and then silently turned and looked out across the water as if she were sizing up my request. She was silent for at least a minute (I had doubtless backed her into a corner, for to decline now would only prove that she was indeed angry) before she turned toward me and, smiling sweetly, replied that it might be a nice idea. "But," she added just as pleasantly, shifting the camera behind her back, "who's going to do it? The camera doesn't have a timer and no one's around to take the picture for us." She smiled broadly now, a smile that seemed tinged with malice, and motioned with her free hand to prove that we were indeed the only people around.

"Good point," I replied, momentarily feeling that she won this battle. "Say," I said, when another idea came to mind, "perhaps I can hold it with one hand and get both of us in a close up?" I raised my right hand in the air in front of both of us to demonstrate where I would hold the camera.

She took a step back as if I were about to do something crazy. "No way," she said adamantly. "We're not going to play with my camera. One misstep and there's several thousand dollars down the toilet."

There was nothing left to say. For me to insist now would only justify her concerns that I couldn't be trusted with her expensive toy. It was beginning to seem that I not only lost the battle but also the war. I was ready to wave the white flag when an elderly Japanese couple appeared almost out of nowhere (actually, from around the corner, which was hidden by some weather-beaten trees) and strolled over to where we were standing. They couldn't speak English very well, but they were able to communicate their desire to have one of us take their picture as they stood with their backs to the ocean. Using hand signs and a few broken English words, the man indicated that he would be happy to reciprocate by taking our picture in the same place – the very spot where I wanted to take our picture. It seemed as if the tide of war was now flowing back in my direction.

Chapter 6

I motioned to the couple that I would be happy to take their picture, and, as they positioned themselves (smiling broadly as if they were young lovers), Luce quietly moved behind me. It's funny, but I could almost feel her simmering and shooting daggers with her eyes into my back. After I had taken the picture and returned their camera, the man and woman bowed politely several times and the man, a silver-haired gentleman with an ingratiating smile, politely motioned to Luce to hand him her camera so that he could reciprocate.

Happily stepping aside, I looked at Luce and could see that she had the look of someone being put on the spot. Not willing to pitch a fit in front of strangers, she carefully balanced the case in her hand, slowly extracted the camera and reluctantly handed it to the man, who smiled and bowed to confirm his acceptance of the precious object. The man's English seemed to be weaker than initially appeared, and so Luce insisted (either to spite me or to discourage the man from using it) on showing him how to hold the camera, how to look through the viewfinder, and how not to touch its various dials – and she did so using a kind of pidgin English that would have been horrifying had their English been a little better. "Me showie you how real camera works, you sabby?" she said at one point, after which the man smiled pleasantly to indicate that he understood her. The man graciously took it all in stride, smiling and bowing at practically every one of her insulting statements. I knew he was only being polite, for he had an expensive camera of his own and the manner in which he handled it suggested that he was quite adept with them.

I had no idea that Luce was such a fine actress. She smiled pleasantly for the picture, and she appeared reasonably pleased to be standing next to me while our images were recorded for posterity. She returned the man's bow when he returned her camera, smiling and bowing again for good measure, as though it had been her honor for him to use it. When everything was said and done, she stepped over to the couple and engaged them in a friendly but rudimentary conversation about their homeland and Carmel, this time without the insulting lingo that peppered her photography instructions.

I came over to them, too, and we all chattered about the water, the cliffs, the trees, and everything else around us using a variety of smiles, hand signals, and simple words. We learned that the couple was from a small town on the coast of Okinawa and that their only son, who recently graduated college, was no longer at home (to tell the truth, it was hard to tell if he had graduated or was about to graduate, although I'm positive that he was probably male). We also learned (I think) that they were both retired and, judging by their clothes and the man's expensive camera, fairly well off. Luckily, we didn't have to describe our relationship, since I'm not sure what signs we could have used to suggest that we were lovers. Maybe it was obvious. But when I tried to say something about my profession, Luce immediately cut me off, using some meaningless hand signals and uttering a drawn-out "boring," which made the couple laugh, as if they too knew how taxing professional people can be if allowed to talk about their work. Luce pointed back to the water, seagulls, and the rest to indicate a better topic of conversation.

We conversed a few more minutes and, when we finally ready to leave, they motioned for another round of pictures, the first with their camera and the second with Luce's. They wanted another shot in front of the ocean and then another with the four of us, which they took by setting their camera on the rock and using the camera's timer. This time Luce surrendered her precious artifact to the gentleman with good grace (not a single word or sign on how to use it), and he not only took one of Luce and me but also one of the four of us. It turned out that Luce's camera did have an auto timer, and she wasn't the least bit surprised when the man placed it on the rock and set the timer going. Well, after this pleasant interlude, we all made our bows and they continued on their way, while Luce and I immediately headed back to the car. We were both a little tired at this point and ready to get something to eat.

The trek back to the car took about fifteen minutes. The path was so narrow, especially when it meandered toward the edge of the cliff, that we were forced to walk single file almost the entire way, or at least until we reached the clearing with the car. I wanted to chat with Luce about the couple, the pictures taken with both cameras, and of course about the scenery – about anything, in fact, just to hear her voice and hopefully catch a smile on her beautiful features. But it was pointless to exchange more than a few ambiguous glances. The wind had picked up, and the air currents swirling around us would have snatched the words out of our mouths. And then there were the seagulls – every time the wind seemed to wane, they would appear overhead practically within reach and screech madly as though they were trying to silence us. Of course, these were minor annoyances, and I had no reason to think that anything was wrong or that she wasn't as pleasant and as cheerful as her face appeared to indicate whenever I glanced back at her. By the time we reached the car, however, something seemed to come over Luce because she seemed sullen and a little edgy. Once inside where it was much quieter, I tried to find out what if anything was troubling her, but she turned away and, resting her chin on her fist, stared out the passenger window.

"What's the matter?" I asked again a few moments later, doing my best to sound concerned. For a couple of seconds, I thought that I had misread her and that she was simply in a thoughtful mood, maybe even a little sad having taken leave of the charming couple and the amazing scenery. But when she still failed to respond, I decided to interrupt her solitude to ask her if there was anything I could do.

"No," she responded callously. "Let's just get out of here."

I started the engine, and as I began negotiating the car onto the road, I tried to make small talk in order to revive what appeared to have been a pleasant interlude.

"Weren't they a great couple?" I asked, feeling certain that she felt the same about them as I did. "The man was really funny. I could have asked him to do almost anything, and I'm sure he would have been happy to oblige. If I told him that I needed help blocking the road, I'm sure he would have lent a hand without a single question. I liked his wife, too, though she was reserved. Maybe it's the culture. I don't know much about it, but I wouldn't mind visiting their country and even them, if they invited us. Who knows? Maybe they did and we didn't understand. What do you think? Weren't they a charming couple? Weren't they? Weren't they?"

Luce was silent.

"What's the matter, sweetheart? Didn't you like them? I thought they were great."

She turned slowly toward me and responded coolly. "They were wonderful. How much more do we need to say about them?"

We reached a fork in the road. Without consulting her, I took the one on the left. Even though we still had some miles to go and lots of beautiful scenery to see before we reached the ranger's station (the drive was one big loop that ended where it began), I thought it best to continue to the hotel without stopping. Luce didn't seem to be in the mood for more water and rocks, and I hoped that the gently-swaying ride back might actually have a soothing effect on her. If worse came to worse, once we got to the hotel, we could take a short nap, get some dinner, and then spend a relaxing evening in our room. But when I glanced at Luce, I could see that her strange mood had deepened (she wasn't always very adept at disguising her feelings), and so I threw caution to the wind and tried to find out what was actually on her mind.

"Are you mad at me? What's the matter?"

"Oh, you know what it is," she said, barely able to control the trembling outrage in her voice.

I was startled by the vehemence of her words. Glancing at her, I was even more surprised by the way she was looking at me. Her beautiful facial features seemed hard and bitter, and I could have sworn that she was mouthing something obscene at me. I was taken aback and didn't know what to say or how to respond.

"Don't play dumb with me," she practically shouted when I didn't immediately respond. "Don't treat me like a child. You know damn well what I'm talking about."

"What? No, I mean...what? I don't have the slightest idea what you're talking about."

"You don't, huh? That's rich." Luce said something at this point that sounded like an epithet, but I couldn't quite grasp it because a large SUV swooped around us and the noise it made obscured what she had said. Either the SUV or the word (or words) made her hesitate for a moment, perhaps giving her an excuse to catch her breath before launching into what was troubling her. "Rich...didn't I tell you that I didn't want to take those pictures? And what makes you think that anything has changed because of that idiotic couple? Oh, they were so cute, weren't they [she said this with a low, mocking tone], all smiles and acting like someone's benevolent grandparents. They were probably making fun of us – especially you – in their language, and they're probably still having fun at our expense right now. So you don't know what I'm talking about, huh?"

"You're upset because the man used your camera, and you think they're laughing at us for some reason?"

"Oh, shut up," she hissed and turned away from me.

"Wait a minute. I'm sorry, but I don't understand any of this. I didn't think they were making fun of us. But it doesn't matter if they were. As for taking pictures with your camera, I thought it was okay with you. You could have said no. I don't understand why you're upset about any of this."

"You don't? You're telling me you don't understand?" She was silent for a second, probably waiting for my answer. When it didn't come (I didn't know what to say), she continued with even more vehemence. "If you don't, you're a bigger..."

I didn't catch the noun, because I was momentarily distracted by all the cars honking at me. Paying attention to her, I had taken my eyes off the road and barely missed colliding with an oncoming car. Luce, however, continued shouting before I had a chance to recover mentally from this slip.

"It's my camera, damn you. I didn't want to take any of those pictures, not of you and not of them. And I certainly didn't want Mr. I'm-such-a-nice-old-fool's dirty fingerprints all over it. Didn't I make myself clear that I didn't want to use my camera? Didn't I say no when you asked, no when you asked again, and no when you tried to steal it out from under my nose? Is there some reason you don't understand no? No, no, no! It's a principle with me. Don't you have any principles?" She growled something else, but it, too, was lost by another car horn. "Watch the road, you fool."

I'm no fool, and I do indeed have principles, and one of them is not to fight while driving. Acting on this principle, I began looking for a suitable spot to pull over so we could have a calmer, more rational discussion of the matter. I also wanted time to understand the problem, since I really couldn't grasp why a simple photograph could have elicited such a monumental reaction. Neither of us said another word until I located a suitable clearing on the side of the road and began angling toward it. It was then that Luce suddenly became animated and informed me that "unless you want more trouble than you can handle, you would be well advised to head directly to the hotel." Naturally, I did as she charmingly requested and swerved back into traffic (to the consternation of the driver behind us, who acted as if he had finally had enough of my inconsistent and dangerous antics on the road). Since the hotel was still a good thirty minutes away, I let Luce stew in silence for twenty of them before tepidly inquiring if she would be interested in getting something to eat before we reached our hotel. With a voice that was struggling to remain calm, she informed me that she wanted to go straight to the hotel and that she wasn't in the least bit hungry, as "our adventures" (her words) left a "bad taste" in her mouth.

Since I didn't respond to any of the horn blowers on the road, I hope you will excuse me if I toot my own horn a little. I am a fairly even-tempered person, and I don't know anyone apart from Luce who would suggest otherwise. While driving, for instance, I rarely experience the kind of tension that many of my fellow travelers do (illustrated by their horns, foul language, and obscene gestures), because I don't get wrapped up in someone else' mistakes or aggressiveness. I realized long ago that such anger is fruitless and often destructive, for what happens on the road are generally innocent mistakes or the result of poor judgment – and without exception we all make numerous mistakes the instant we travel five feet by car or ten on foot, even if it's only to the local market. It's therefore unconscionable to me to berate (or worse) someone for doing the very same thing that I have done in other circumstances. Look, nobody's perfect, and because I recognize this salient fact of human nature, I am a little calmer than most people and, not to brag, a little more forgiving of human foibles. Let's be clear: I have my weaknesses, but I can certainly control my emotions a lot better than Luce can control hers. But having said this, I also have to admit that the ugliness of her behavior, her inexplicable and childish tantrums, unexpectedly set me on edge and as a result I said nothing else to her until the moment we arrived at the hotel.

Needless to say, I was physically and emotionally drained by the time we parked. I was also hungry, ravenously so, despite the knots in my stomach caused by her behavior, but I was reluctant to broach the subject of food (I didn't know how she would react to something so elemental) and instead hoped that she would bring the subject up after we checked in. Food, I prayed, would be the territory over which we could make peace.

Chapter 7

The Hacienda Plantation, as our hotel and its grounds were called, looked nothing like a hacienda or a plantation. The incongruity of the name was accentuated by the quaint Victorian look of the building, which was a pale green, three-story edifice with two large, white pillars framing the front door, and by the flower gardens (tulips, maybe, although I don't know a thing about flowers and wasn't ready to venture a question about them to Luce) that covered most of the grounds. If I retained any doubts about the advisability of this trip, they were more or less gone when I finished soaking up the beauty of this place. In fact, by the time we entered the lobby, which exuded a warmth characteristic of certain periods in the 19th century (there were oil paintings on every wall depicting men with muttonchops, women with hoop skirts, and children playing croquet on immaculately trimmed lawns) and silently picked up our keys at the front desk, I was ready to put everything behind us and, if she demanded, drop to my knees and beg for forgiveness, even though I wasn't the cause of the problems. I was fortunately spared such debasement, for even though we hobbled up the stairs with the suitcases in complete silence (I hobbled, since Luce refused to carry anything except her purse and that blasted camera), the instant we reached the room things changed and Luce appeared calm and relaxed. She even managed to smile at something, curling the ends of her lips in that lovely, enticing way she had.

How do I describe the room and thus what seemed to be the reason for Luce's sudden change of heart? Well, it was pretty much like the rest of the hotel. It was decorated with prints of horses and fox hunts, and in the center, dominating the room, was a large, four-poster bed that was covered by a thick, lacy quilt which appeared to have been made from one of those hoop-skirts from the previous century. While intensely eyeing the bed, Luce quietly informed me that she wasn't hungry (the owner mentioned room service and a restaurant around the corner as he pointed to the stairs) and claimed (yawning at the same time) that the only she thing she wanted to do was to snuggle into bed and get a good night's sleep.

I have to say that overstuffed bed with its huge pillows certainly looked appealing, especially after the long and stressful drive. But what looked even more appealing was Luce herself, as she briefly sat down on the bed and tested its softness, after which she fluffed up both of the pillows. Despite my stomach's objections and the fact that it was still light outside (it was a little after six, and I rarely go to bed before eleven), I was ready to forgo any number of minor inconveniences to spend the rest of the night with this beautiful and, once again, desirable woman.

We fumbled around for a few minutes after this, opening our suitcases and dispersing our personal items in the closets and dressers, after which I mentioned the bathroom and getting ready for bed. Luce smiled in her sweet, alluring way and silently, graciously motioned me to the bathroom first – and, as I took one last glance at her beautiful face and charmingly disheveled hair (she had just run both hands through it), I couldn't help thinking that I was truly in love and that despite our minor disagreement earlier, this was the beginning of something very special for both of us.

Sometimes, though, things are not as innocent as they seem. While I was in the bathroom getting ready for what I hoped would be a lively and rewarding evening (washing my hands and face, brushing my teeth and hair, and donning a pair of black silk pajamas purchased specifically for this trip), Luce was in the other room quietly repacking and closing her bags. She was gone by the time I stepped out of the bathroom. I'm still surprised that I didn't hear the door shut after her, and when I looked out the window there was no evidence of her anywhere. I suppose she caught a cab or shuttle somewhere, but where she went after that was anyone's guess. I'd like to imagine that she had some qualms about leaving, maybe about sticking me with the bill, but the manner in which she left suggested that whatever qualms she did have, they weren't about me. You know, I could never decide what I found more surprising about this little event – the fact that she left me or the fact that she was able to do it so quickly.

A few minutes later I found something that surprised me almost as much as Luce's unexpected departure, something that at first seemed totally inexplicable. As I turned away from the window and walked toward the bed, I noticed Luce's fancy camera nestled snugly in its brown leather case and sitting neatly in the center of the bed. At first, I thought she left it there by accident in her rush to get away. The idea that she had forgotten the thing – the precious gem that was the source of our biggest problems – struck me as both ironic and laughable. What was even funnier was the idea that she would have to contact me to get it back (and after what had happened, I wasn't about to contact her or spend a few measly bucks mailing it back to her) – me, the very person she was escaping from and, judging by her haste, probably the last person in the world she wanted to contact. Rolling everything over in my mind and practically rolling on the floor with laughter because of her predicament, it suddenly occurred to me that the camera hadn't been left by accident. No, she left it on purpose. It was obvious when I noticed the care with which she had placed the camera upright in the very center of the bed – it was a clear message that she would rather have parted from her expensive camera than spend another second with me.

Unable to laugh or cry, I grabbed the camera and was about to chuck it into the trash bin (my considered response to her heartless statement) when I realized that such an item was too valuable, too useful, to toss away willy-nilly. Besides, she wanted me to toss it, I told myself, because it was tantamount to a divorce agreement that could only be consummated if signed by such an act. But as I thought about it a little more, I realized that if I kept the camera – and used it – it would prove (to me, at least) that I was above her kind of rash, juvenile behavior and that she couldn't dictate the terms of anything to me, much less a symbolic divorce. My first act of defiance, therefore, was to turn on the camera. Emboldened by its immediate response, my second was to see if the pictures were still there. I half-expected her to have erased them, which would have been a convenient way to eliminate something unpleasant and, at the same time, strike another defiant blow against me. But this wasn't the case. The pictures were there, and it was obvious that she didn't care enough about me to waste her precious time eliminating either the past or her own unpleasantness. Even the image of that stupid weed was there, its pathetic leaves glistening in the sunlight and mocking the fact that Luce chose to memorialize it rather than me. Well, it did offer a certain degree of aesthetic pleasure when I erased it.

"So, that's that," I said bravely, as I sat down on the bed and placed the camera on the night stand. Since it was too late to leave, I decided to spend at least one night in this love nest (after, of course, ordering dinner) before making my lonely way back to the Bay Area. It would have been nice to stay at least a few days, I told myself, but what sort of fun could one have in this town alone and without anything particular to do? However, as I considered my situation over a pleasant repast of steak and Maine lobster and an expensive bottle of wine, I realized that there were plenty of things to do in Carmel with or without a special someone and, more importantly, I realized that if I left too soon I would be falling into a trap – that is, ruining my vacation because she ruined hers, and I didn't doubt that she wanted me to be as unhappy as she was. I decided to stay the rest of the week, just as I had initially planned, and throughout this time I would see and do everything that I wanted to see and do with Luce. Despite my earlier concerns, by the time I was finished with my supper I was actually looking forward to this time by myself.

Chapter 8

The week turned out much better than I expected. As I noted, I intended doing everything that I planned to do with Luce (minus some things), which meant that as soon as I got up in the morning, I would head directly to the beach and spend most of the day lounging in the sun and splashing in the waves. In fact, I intended to do that, but when I opened the door of my room and looked into the wood-paneled hallway, I changed my mind and decided to do everything that interested me, not what would have pleased a certain person.

Instead of the beach, I went to the center of the town and spent the entire day combing through the shops and galleries, admiring this and that and occasionally speaking to local artists. From one of the smaller galleries, I bought a small sailboat molded out of copper and, from one of the clothing stores, I purchased a couple of tee-shirts that said "Carmel USA" on the front. I also picked up a number of odds and ends from some other shops (a newspaper, some magazines, a couple of souvenirs with Carmel emblazoned on the front and "Made in Taiwan" etched on the back, a tube of expensive toothpaste, and so on), and later that evening I ate at one of the nice restaurants just up the street from the water. I don't remember the name of the establishment, but I still vividly recall the seafood linguine, especially the scallops, which still make my mouth salivate when I think of them. The following days were more or less the same, and each evening I trudged back to the hotel, tired and interested in little else than a good night's sleep. On the final night, I went to a nightclub, if you could call it that (it was actually a restaurant that on certain nights featured a live jazz trio), and stayed there for hours, listening to the music and occasionally speaking to some of the guests. I don't remember much about it other than the cigarette smoke, although I distinctly recall slogging back to the hotel and collapsing on the bed, where I fought off the beginnings of a hangover.

Nevertheless, I was up early the following morning and ready for the drive home. Maybe this isn't exactly correct. I was up early, all right, but because I ended up having had such a good time – much better than I could have had with Luce – I was reluctant to leave and return to the hum-drum world of everyday life. I couldn't stay any longer away from work, although I did prolong my vacation a little by taking the long way back, the very route that Luce and I had taken to get to Carmel, and allowed myself the pleasure of enjoying the sights and smells that I had missed when I was with her. I even spent an extra forty minutes at the very produce stand that had occasioned one of our early arguments, leaving with a couple baskets of artichokes and a greater appreciation of the surrounding area's natural attractions. It was a peaceful, pleasant drive, and I somehow managed to return home while the sun was up and with enough time to relax (a vacation from the vacation) before going to the office the following day.

You know, throughout this entire time, from the instant that I first walked out of my hotel determined to see Carmel until my return home, I thought very little about Luce. Well, I did think of her from time to time (I wouldn't have been human if I didn't) but not in anger and especially not with desire. I was past such emotions. I simply considered her in passing as I might have considered almost anyone else, and I couldn't help feeling little more than pity for this absurd individual. By the time I had been home for a couple of hours, though, long enough to get a drink and settle into a nice, deep-cushioned chair on my patio, I reflected on my former relationship with her. Even then I wasn't angry. True, I wanted nothing to do with her ever again, but at the same time I didn't mind thinking about her, just a little. I wanted to remember the way she looked – her dark eyes, her blond hair, her smooth skin – and the way she smelled, almost like roses, which of course was due to the moisturizing cream she slathered over her lovely body. Sometimes I've wondered if I fell for Luce simply because of her amazing beauty, but as I visualized her from various angles, I realized that my attraction to her went well beyond such superficiality. Indeed, there was something else about her

34

personality, something apart from her quirky mood swings and her often demeaning taunts, that was alluring and at times made me want to touch her, possess her as if she were a piece of great art hidden beyond reach in a glass case. I dozed off before I could figure out what it was.

Chapter 9

I had been home for a couple weeks or so when I heard again from Luce. It must have been about two in the morning when she phoned, although I am not positive about the exact time since I was more asleep than awake. But the second I heard the dulcet tone asking for Reeky (which for some reason she pronounced rolling the 'r'), I knew it was her and I also knew she wanted something (why else would she call if not to retrieve her precious camera?). Imagine my delight when the camera wasn't mentioned once during our hour-long conversation. Luce seemed to have forgotten the camera, or else it was no longer an object of interest to her. No, what she wanted was me – she called to see if we could get back together.

"Reeky, Reeky, please," she practically cried (never failing to roll the 'r'), "I am so sorry for my behavior. It was inexcusable. I don't know what was wrong with me. You have to believe me, it wasn't you. Not my Reeky. You were perfect. Others could see it, too. Reeky, Reeky, I was a monster…please, it's true….and you of all people didn't deserve such abuse."

I was dumbfounded, and not because I had just been awoken from a comfortable sleep. I had never heard Luce apologize for anything before, and here she was taking complete responsibility for the failure of our Carmel trip. Not only that, she sounded desperate (her voice had an edgy quality to it, and there were times when she stumbled on words and choked on others), which was not only a revelation but completely unlike the angry, snarling person I had known before and during Carmel.

"Please, please, please, Reeky," she said, sniffling every now and then, "please, you must forgive me. You don't know how sorry I am for my behavior. I don't know what to do if you won't open your heart for me just a little."

Luce wasn't drunk (I could tell from the way she articulated certain words, including my name, and from the overall clarity of her diction) and in fact seemed eminently rational, which admittedly was hard to accept in the middle of the night wearing black, silk pajamas. "I don't know what to say. Reeky, you are very quiet. Please speak to me. Did I wake you? No?"

Even though I was exhausted, I knew that I should have hung up or least let her know that her insensitive, possibly psychotic behavior hurt me deeply. If nothing else, I should have insisted on discussing her behavior later in the day, after a solid night's sleep, when I was able to think more clearly. But for some reason I couldn't. I couldn't bring myself to be so heartless, not in the middle of a dark night while wearing pajamas, and so after a few more minutes of listening to her self-flagellation, I found myself assuaging her pain, calming her, and letting her know that I had already forgiven everything. Shortly after that I even shouldered some of the blame.

"I'm at fault, too," I added magnanimously, and then felt a little stupid when she immediately agreed. But who knows? Perhaps I was a little insistent on some things, and maybe I could have handled the incident at the produce stand a little better. And then there was the camera – did I really have to insist on a photograph? And the nice couple who took our photograph – couldn't I have intervened in some way to prevent the man from reaching for the camera? Had I done that, maybe things would have blown over, and we would have had a fine time on the beach. Naturally, I didn't say any of this and kept my half-hearted apologies abstract and nonspecific.

The conversation finally ended after I promised to call her later in the week. I was glad that the air had been cleared, but at the same time I wished that I hadn't been quite so noble and that we both had agreed that she had been a real jerk.

The following day, after wrestling with a tricky set of investments for a special customer, I looked up from my desk and, closing my eyes briefly, wondered if we would be better off if I didn't call. I had no doubt about her beauty, and there was something intriguing about her personality, but I also realized that if we continued along this path, the whole, crazy affair could begin again, along with the anger, the mood swings, the psychosis, and I don't know what else. Not only that, I was also concerned that the camera would again raise its ugly Teutonic head, and I wasn't prepared to deal with that. Shaking my head and then massaging a couple of numbers here and there to make the pieces of the financial puzzle fit together better, I knew that I shouldn't call too soon, since I was still angry over the beginning of the Carmel trip and with myself for shouldering some of the blame. By the time I arrived home, I was determined to wait until I could laugh off Carmel and all the rest before calling her – and if it turned out that I never found anything funny about it, then that would be for the best. My plan dissolved in thin air minutes later when the phone rang and I heard her cooing my name, or nickname, since she rarely called me by my proper name.

Oh, how I adored the sound of her voice. Even though she was born and bred in this country, she sometimes spoke as if she were an Italian or a Spaniard, mangling my name and adding a motorboat sound to the very first letter. I didn't care, for her voice no longer sounded harsh but was soft and tinged with regret and sadness.

We must have been on the phone for at least an hour before the conversation became serious. Prior to that, we spoke about everything under the sun – speaking as if Carmel didn't exist – the weather, for example, our apartments, my job (she was still in between positions of some kind), and so forth – but as we became more relaxed, things subtly started to change and we began baring our souls, so to speak. Without providing specifics, I told her about certain changes in a client's package that I was required to make to improve his tax base – changes, I explained, that I didn't feel comfortable making. Of course, I was a team player, but I wasn't going to take one for the team, if it came to that. Puzzled, Luce immediately launched into an incident that happened only a few days ago (after Carmel but before the first call) that apparently changed her life and altered her attitude toward me.

She was driving home on the highway one evening after visiting a sick friend and was nearly "annihilated" (her word) by an enormous truck and trailer (she added that the trailer alone was as long as a city block). It was nearly midnight, and a steady rain had been falling for hours, severely hampering visibility and making the highway as slick as ice. In fact, despite the "heroic" (again, her word) efforts of her maniacally flailing wipers, she could barely see the traffic around her, especially when the lights from oncoming traffic burst into thousands of little dancing bubbles across the windshield. At any rate, when she sensed her exit coming up, she carefully maneuvered her car into the far-right lane and slowed down so that when the time came she could ease off the highway without hydroplaning past the ramp. Everything was going as expected – the car was under control because she was driving well within her capabilities – when the aforementioned truck and trailer arose out of nowhere like a gigantic black mountain and swooped past her on the right (off the road), its horn screaming and the turbulence from the trailer buffeting her little car and engulfing it in an ocean of roiling water. Using every ounce of skill she had, Luce somehow managed to keep the car from swimming in the truck's wake and either crashing into a road barrier or another car.

Luce told me that once the mountainous truck disappeared around the corner, she eased off the throttle and began edging the car off the road. She wanted to bring to the car to a stop so that she could take a few minutes to calm her nerves. But just as she began lightly applying the brakes, the car suddenly went into a spin and began propelling her toward the edge of an overpass and almost certain death. By sheer luck, the car hit a divot in the road and changed directions, this time spinning across the road to the left, narrowly missing the overpass and some oncoming vehicles, and came to a soft thud against a traffic barrier. It was surprising that she hadn't hit anything along the way, and what seemed even more surprising was that by the time she came to her senses (a matter of seconds), the car's engine was purring, the wipers going full blast, and nothing seemed out of the ordinary. Like her car, she seemed to have come through everything relatively unscathed albeit a bit rattled (sometime later she discovered some bruises on her ankles and feet that must have come from desperately working the car's pedals).

Luce remained where she was for several minutes (again, she needed to calm her nerves). When she was ready to resume driving, she noticed that the rain had stopped and that the moon's soft light was leaching through the dark clouds, offering enough light to see the highway in front of her. And it was only then, she emphasized with an emotionally-charged tremor in her voice, that she noticed her car was in the wrong lane and facing the oncoming traffic (which was slowing down to look and honk at her) and that she had escaped plummeting off the opposite side of the overpass by mere inches – a nudge would have sent her downward some thirty feet to the traffic below.

Realizing how close she had been to the "Big D" (she couldn't say death) – and not just once but apparently several times during the same incident – Luce began to feel lighthearted and giddy. No, she didn't start singing bawdy songs or begin dancing a tango on the hood of her car. But she did feel a "tingling" in her lips and shortly afterwards noticed the tops of her cheeks in the corners of her eyes. Yes, she was smiling, and smiling as if she had heard something wildly amusing. After a few minutes of this restrained euphoria, a sensation of calmness permeated her "very being" and she came back to earth (her words) – she had cheated Mr. D and, as a result, she realized that her life would never again be the same. Even though she apparently didn't ask herself why life needed to be different, she nevertheless decided that henceforth she would dedicate her existence "to the good, to the true, and to the..." something else, which at the moment slips my mind.

Having somehow managed to cross the highway and get back into the correct lanes, Luce felt confident and steady, even though the road conditions had continued to deteriorate (the moon was again obscured by dark clouds and the rain had come back, at times ferociously) and the car was now slipping and sliding with increasing frequency. A little closer to home, the car veered off the road when she couldn't negotiate a curve, and it wallowed in the mud and water like a pig before she was able to coax it back onto the pavement – and this minor experience, with its echoes of the first, helped drive home the point that things can be lost forever in the blinking of an eye. As a result, Luce not only promised some vague being to focus her life on the good, the true, and the whatever, but she also gave her word to appreciate the things (life, naturally, as well as friends, places, and her absurd troll-doll collection, which she had been amassing since grade school) while she had them and not toss them aside without good cause. I should note that her new attitude toward life and things didn't include the driver of the big rig. She couldn't decide whether she wanted him eviscerated or castrated. But by the time she arrived home, she was too tired and too grateful for other things to worry about that "loser."

Apparently, she went to sleep almost immediately. She told me that she remembered falling gently on her pillow but nothing after that. Well, almost nothing. Sometime later in the night, she jerked awake, bathed in sweat and nearly paralyzed with fear. She was having trouble breathing, and her heart was beating so violently that she was afraid it would rip out of her chest and disappear into the suffocating darkness engulfing her. Once she came to her senses, she realized that she was on edge because of a nightmare, although she couldn't recall a single detail. However, she was now wide awake and unable to close her eyes, even for a couple of seconds, and so she remained motionless, lying on her back and staring into the fathomless darkness overhead. Sometime later on (and she had lost all sense of time), a glimmer of light arose on the horizon of her consciousness and, once again, she realized just how close she had come to Mickey D. But instead of confronting this realization with the equanimity that comes from familiar surroundings, she became depressed and then riotously angry, cursing the driver, the truck, the road, the rain, the night, and everything else that had contributed to her unfortunate experience. It was only after a faint light began peeping between the curtains that her strained emotions calmed and, after some "soul searching" (again, her words), she decided to put the past behind her and "get on with the business of life."

Now, even if I didn't buy into everything she said (some of it was a little too contrived), it still had the ring of truth, given the way she was speaking to me and the soothing sound of her voice. Would she have been able to forgive the truck driver or at least forget him so that her new life could begin unencumbered by a painful, unpleasant moment in the past? Probably not; that would have been pushing things a bit. But because her story illustrated the weaknesses of her character as much as its strengths, I could feel myself being drawn to her in a way that was completely different than the last time we were together. My feelings for her became stronger and less focused on her beauty. It sounds silly, but her vulnerability appealed to me, and it spoke to an innate desire to console and forgive. I don't know, but it's fair to say that something began to stir in me that was different than my previous feelings for her. Within days of the call, we were again fast friends. No – we were lovers in every sense of the word.

We didn't move in together, but we did manage to occupy the same bed (mine) once or twice a week. We also spent an inordinate amount of time together. Sometimes we spent the better part of a weekend snuggling on my couch (hers was too small and too fragile), relaxing, sleeping, and watching TV, especially the mind-numbing reality shows that attracted her like a magnet. Sometimes we spent the evening out, sampling fine restaurants (as long as I paid) and going to the movies. Luce loved the movies, and I never met anyone so attentive to the nuances of a plot or the facets of a character. On one occasion, she laughed practically nonstop through some moronic comedy, pausing from time to time to inform me that if she continued laughing she might pee her pants. On another occasion, we endured a sensitive saga about wartime refugees as they migrated from the frozen wastes of somewhere to the frozen wastes of somewhere else. Luce wept from the movie's unfortunate beginning to its bitter end, and at no place more intensely than during the final scene where the old man (his brains addled by the explosion of a nearby mortar round) and his wife (who suffered from an incurable wound caused by the same round) dragged a broken wheelbarrow into a blizzard, where they faded from view to the sounds of nuns singing children's songs. I couldn't tell you what this nonsense was supposed to mean, but it certainly affected Luce who, when the credits were mercifully over, spit out a series of invectives against the people who inflicted such unhappiness on Ma and Pa Kettle (the truck driver may also have borne some responsibility). In a sense, it affected me, too, as it enabled me to console her without putting my clean clothes in jeopardy. So, when we weren't eating together, sleeping together, or enjoying the visual arts together, we chatted up a storm by phone or email.

Chapter 10

A few months later, my feelings for her intensified quite unexpectedly. And I remember the exact moment when this happened. It was Friday evening, and I hadn't seen or heard from Luce in nearly four days. Having eaten and tidied up the kitchen, I was now sitting alone in my dark living room, holding my phone and waiting for Luce to call. I had no particular reason to expect her call, we hadn't made any plans to communicate that evening, and yet I couldn't help feeling that she was going to call me, quite possibly within the next few minutes. When that didn't happen, and after I waited there for another couple hours anticipating her familiar ring, I unaccountably felt lost, anxious, bereft of the desire to do anything until I heard her soft, gentle voice – and it was then, at this very instant, after hours of sitting impatiently in the darkness, that I realized I couldn't live without her, that life without this wonderful, quirky individual wasn't life at all but a mere charade, a stupid, pointless game. With a clarity resembling revelation, I knew that I was finally, hopelessly in love.

How can I explain this in a way that makes sense? Luce had changed, and for the most part she had ceased to be the brooding, obdurate individual who tried to make our lives miserable in Carmel. The chance encounter with a big rig softened her and turned her into a gentle, caring individual who was often a joy to be around. Sure, she had her moments, but she quickly recognized them and laughed them off as easily as I did. On the other hand, the feeling was new to me; I have been infatuated with many women but never once felt anything like this – it was like a gigantic ocean wave washing over me, threatening to drown me, unless she reached out and saved me with the very words that I longed to say to her. No, there was no doubt about it, I was in love; and as I waited for that damned phone to ring, I could see her beautiful face, the gentle curves of her arms as they held each other, and the manner in which she balanced on one leg and used the foot of the other to tap out her impatience. I couldn't resist reaching out to caress her soft cheeks and lips, but just as the tips of my fingers were a fraction of an inch away from her flesh, she burst into a million tiny stars that quickly faded into the black night. Awakened by an insistent rumble from my phone, I fumbled desperately with its slick case until I managed to flick it open before the final ring. "Luce," I cried desperately, "you can't believe how much I wanted to talk to you."

"This ain't Luce, bro," someone said on the other end. The caller had a coarse, masculine baritone, and his cocky insolence seemed to be mocking my predicament. It was a telemarketer, of course, and I shouted some obscenities at the unfortunate individual before hurling the phone against the opposite wall, where in exploded in jumble of little pieces.

Desperate, unable to call her, I decided to make a mad dash to her apartment to talk to her (actually, I took my car, for while her place was only a few miles away, the roads leading there crept over some of the most mountainous parts of the city, making any walk a time-consuming, strenuous exercise). Even though Luce and I had been lovers for a relatively short period of time, I now felt as if I had known her all my life and so it seemed quite reasonable to speak to her now before another hour, minute, or second was lost. Glancing at my watch (it was nearly ten o'clock) as I slipped behind the wheel, it occurred to me that it might be a little late to be calling now, and yet I couldn't hold back. I told myself that she would almost certainly be awake when I arrived and that she could relax and go back to sleep once we spoke. It was after one o'clock when I reached her building (traffic in San Francisco can be unpredictable).

The door to her building was locked when I arrived, and there was no way getting inside without buzzing her and waking some of the other tenants. Naturally, I would have pounded on that shiny little button – I would have risked waking every person in the building – but only if I had been certain that she was still awake and waiting for me. Nothing seemed to be stirring in her apartment. It was on the third floor (too high to reach by ordinary means), but the living room window looked onto the sidewalk where I was standing. From where I stood, I could have detected even the feeblest light emanating from the living room and practically everywhere else in the place, but all was dark and so I reluctantly decided to leave and let everyone get a decent night's sleep. Before I left, however, I stepped closer to the brass-plated callbox which was glistening in the bright moonlight. Staring at Luce's button, I couldn't resist the impulse to caress its sleek surface, to scratch a spec of dirt off a worn edge with my thumbnail, all the while wondering what might really happen if I put a little pressure on the center of the button. Would it wake the other tenants or just my love? And if it woke the others, would that be so bad – would that be a crime in anyone's eyes? I hesitated, the temptation was almost overpowering, and yet I stepped back before making that irrevocable decision. I wanted to speak to her, but I didn't want to expose my heart at the wrong moment, while she was rubbing her sleepy eyes and her neighbors were threatening to dismember me. Looking once more at the window, seeking in its darkness a reason to push the button, I reluctantly turned away from the building and drove home.

It was nearly three by the time I crawled into my own bed. I was so tired that I could hardly see straight, and yet I had little trouble envisioning Luce's soft, slender neck, her smooth flesh behind the left ear, and her graceful kneecaps, which alternated between a slight stubble and a soft pillow as I fingered each rounded convolution. Stretching on the very bed that she had graced many times, I resolved to tell her everything the following morning, everything that I wanted to say this evening. I would call her the first thing (or perhaps the second thing, since I needed to get a new phone) and ask her to meet me near the windmill in Golden Gate Park, one of the most romantic spots in the city, and while we lounged on the grass eating the gracious meal that I had prepared, I would pour out my heart to her. For a few moments, I could feel her sitting next to me and see her smiling in anticipation of the words I was going to say. Cool ocean breezes swirled around us (the ocean was practically on the other side of the trees) and ruffled her hair, and as I took her into my arms and held her tightly, I practically breathed my love into her precious ear. Pulling the pillow closer to my chest, I thanked the truck driver who made this all possible. Had Luce not been so incensed by the man's mere existence, I could have imagined him at our wedding, standing at the back of the church and nodding in a knowing, satisfied way.

Did I actually dream about Luce that night? I'd like to think so, but the truth is that I don't recall dreaming about anything. I do remember feeling warm all over and, seconds later, thinking in a vague way that this day would be one that I would never forget. Is it possible to describe these sensations, putting into pedestrian words something that suffused my being the moment my eyes met the early morning light peering under the blinds? Probably not. I can only say that shortly after I awoke, I was eager to declare my love and even more anxious to hear Luce say the same to me. But before that could happen, I needed to rush to the store and acquire a new phone. The power of love is amazing, for it induced me to change phone carriers before my current contract expired and shell out an obscene amount for a cheap replacement phone. Regardless, I managed to call her on my way out of the store and made a date for a noon lunch in the park. I have to say that Luce sounded a little cranky on the phone and that her deadpan affirmative could have been construed to mean that she wanted to end the call as quickly as possible. But I knew Luce, and I knew that she wasn't the cheeriest person in the morning, and it didn't matter because this was going to be the day that I declared my love to her.

The day was as bright and lovely as my desire. Since I still had more than two hours before we were to meet at the park, I went from the phone store to a nearby gourmet shop and picked up some special items for our lunch – an assortment of fine hams, cheeses, crackers, and related comestibles, as well as a small tin of caviar, which was a darned sight cheaper than my stupid phone. I also picked up a bottle of expensive red wine and an even pricier bottle of champagne (even these, together with the rest of my fixings, were less than that phone). Back in my apartment, I put everything in order and carefully packed it in a lovely wicker picnic basket that I had purchased some years back but never used. I also added some real silverware (a gift from my late grandmother) and genuine silk napkins that I bought last year for no particular reason (and, if I recall correctly, even the napkins were cheaper than the phone). Securing the lid, I charged out of my apartment and went to the park, where I found a centrally-located spot that was visible from the street. If Luce followed my directions, she couldn't miss me, especially because I tied one of the napkins on a slender stick that I poked into the ground next to the blanket.

This section of the park was practically empty, although I knew that it wouldn't stay this way all day. There were only a couple of people doing something to the ground at the north end, about a hundred yards from where I was sitting, and an old man and his dog to the east, about half that distance away. When the man and his dog got within fifty feet, I was ready to holler at him to take his ugly mutt out of the park (the stupid dog was lifting his leg on everything), but he turned before I could say anything and disappeared into a nearby stand of trees. He didn't reappear, and so I continued straightening out my blanket and placing the food and utensils in strategic places near its center. Since I still had some time, I rearranged everything several times, especially the utensils, to make sure it was all within reach and that Luce had plenty of room to snuggle up to me while we ate and talked.

When things seemed perfect (for the fourth or fifth time), I decided to relax for a few minutes before she arrived. I stretched out on the blanket on my left side and scanned the park and the passing cars for signs of her approach. Since it was still early (she wasn't due for half an hour), I closed my eyes for a few minutes to soak up the warm sun and cool air. Within seconds, I began to imagine how I would break the news. It seemed simple enough. Relaxing on my left side, my arm draped over my right, upraised knee, I would calmly tell her how I came to the twin decisions of loving her and expressing my love. I wouldn't look at her while articulating my decisions, but when I was done I would turn to her and know from her expression that she felt the same about me.

After a while my side began to ache, and I changed position, rolling onto my stomach and propping my head onto both fists. Glancing at my watch, I noticed that she was fifteen minutes late, but instead of standing up and scanning the park for her, I began to think it might be better to rest on my right side while I absently plucked one blade of grass after another with my free hand, tossing each one aside as if it were nothing in the greater scheme of things. After I tossed the last one, I would mutter "enough is enough" and turn to her.

"Look, Luce," I would begin, speaking as though it were finally time to level with one another, "I love you. Surely, you must have known this for some time."

She smiled and nodded eagerly.

"Well, if you ever had any doubt, it's time to put those doubts aside." I stared at her, forcefully but lovingly. "We're too old to play games. Tell me if you love me, too, which I hope is the case; and if you don't, that's fine, too. We can let bygones be bygones."

Choking on her tears, big, glistening drops running down both sides of her cheeks, she carefully enunciated the words I desperately longed to hear. We embraced after that, and rest was, as they say, history.

Chapter 11

I opened my eyes and glanced at my watch. It was nearly one o'clock, and as I looked around the park, she was nowhere in sight. Afraid that something might have happened to delay her, I decided to give her a quick call to see if there was anything I could do. Traffic was a problem everywhere; and despite the fact that there was only one windmill, the park was so large that it was easy to get lost among its roads and grasslands. I ended up redialing the number several times, each time fearing that I had misdialed or that she couldn't pick up in time, but there was still no answer (and her voice box wasn't operational, not that I wanted to leave a message). My concern peaked around two o'clock but then subsided after a few more fruitless phone calls made it clear that she had either forgotten our date or had put it aside for something else. By 2:30, I was annoyed – she couldn't bother coming to the most important date of our lives – and fifteen minutes after that, I started in on one of the sandwiches. Shortly after I finished the sandwich and was about to open the wine, Luce arrived.

She was every bit as beautiful as I expected her to be. Wearing black slacks and a loose fitting, cream-colored silk blouse, she topped off her outfit with black, oversized sunglasses and lovely straw hat to keep the bright sun off her face. But while her face was exquisite (her lips had a peach tone to them that complemented the rest of her features), her expression seemed troubled – her lips were tight and straight – as if there was something serious on her mind.

As I rose to my feet, I asked her if she had trouble finding this place.

Using a firm motion with the palm of her hand, Luce told me to sit back down. "Don't get up on my account. I have to leave in a few minutes," she said coolly.

"What? I thought we could have a nice picnic, and..."

"It's too uncomfortable," she replied, now standing next to me with her back to the sun. It was difficult to look up at her without shielding my eyes from the bright, unpleasant light. "Besides, there are bugs around here."

"Bugs? What bugs? Why do you have to leave so soon? When I spoke to you, I thought we agreed…"

"I don't know what you're babbling about. What do you want to tell me? And I don't know why you couldn't say it over the phone." She glanced at something on the edge of the park and then turned back to me. "Well?"

I was determined not to get upset – even the best laid plans can derail – and so I calmly explained that I invited her out here for a reason. "A very important reason," I added. I mentioned in passing that I had been to her apartment last night.

That statement alone caught her attention. "Really? When? I don't remember seeing you. Maybe you went to the wrong place."

"No, I was there, outside. It was nearly eleven, and all your lights were out."

"I see."

"Actually, it was closer to midnight, and I didn't see the point in waking you at that hour."

"Midnight?"

"Give or take. Maybe later."

She hesitated and appeared to be thinking of something. "It doesn't matter," she replied. "I wasn't home. So, what's so important that you wanted me to come all the way out here to say it? Can't it wait for another day?"

"No, I mean…what? I had a good reason for coming here. It's important."

Luce sighed. Once again, she glanced at something at the edge of the park, but I couldn't see anything. "Okay, keep your shirt on. Say what you need to say and be quick about it. I've got things to do, and this is a complete waste of time."

For a couple of moments, I wasn't entirely certain that I should share everything on my mind, for what was uppermost wasn't my undying love but her rudeness and the fact that she had something better to do than to speak to me. I also wanted to know what she planned to do after she left. "Wait a minute," I said finally, "why can't you stay? What are doing that's so important?"

"If it was any of your business, I'd tell you." Luce hesitated as if she regretted speaking to me this way. "Look," she began in a softer tone, "I'm really late, and I don't like standing in the mud. Why don't we have dinner later, or some other time, and you can tell me what's on your mind. Something smells bad. I'll call you." She mumbled something about the grass and mud and walked away. No good-bye, no kiss, no nothing.

I watched her leave the park, disappearing around the corner where she had evidently parked. Once out of sight, I was tempted to run after her to see if she had been here or if I had imagined the whole, unpleasant event. Yes, I told myself, I must have been dreaming, just as I was dreaming when I imagined how I would break the good news to her, but when I noticed the holes that her heels made in the grass, I knew that she had been here. Oh, how I wished it had been a dream, for I could wake up and laugh at the absurd situation and the uncharacteristic manner in which Luce behaved. Well, at least we could meet for dinner, and despite this drastic turn of events, I was still eager to proclaim my love…sort of. I couldn't understand what she was doing out so late last night and what she could possibly be doing today – or why she couldn't tell me about these things. Putting these things temporarily out of mind, I was fairly confident that she would shed light on them over dinner.

Chapter 12

I spent the rest of the afternoon in my apartment, wandering around, sitting now and then, and wondering why it took her so long to get back to me. Once again, I found my restlessness turning to anger. I really couldn't understand why someone would make someone else wait while the first someone took her sweet time about calling. Couldn't Luce have spared a couple of minutes, one minute – thirty seconds, even – from her busy schedule to give me a ring and set a time? And what could she be doing that was so important? Or, if her day were truly busy, why couldn't she have spared a few seconds to send me a text, noting that this evening was difficult but the next was open? How much time would that take? How much time does ordinary courtesy take? More than once, I was tempted to call her – in one instance, dialing her number before immediately hanging up – but I restrained myself. She said that she would call and I didn't want appear desperate.

I had given up on dinner with her by seven, and so I microwaved some leftovers and ate them while watching a baseball game on TV. The dinner was bland, the game was uninteresting, and when I was done, which was long before the seventh-inning stretch, I went out for a walk to calm my nerves and forget this day ever happened. I would call her tomorrow or the day after, I reassured myself, and in the meantime I started down the street with no particular direction or destination in mind.

Strolling up one street and down another, I looked at the buildings and at the people on the sidewalks like an explorer might look at them, having for the first time stepped foot on this strange, new world. I observed the dirt and grime on the streets, the foul human smell that hovered over everything, and as I turned the corner I noticed the grubbiness of the buildings and the people loitering on the corner, waiting for something that would never come. The neighborhood changed a few blocks after this. The buildings began to get taller, they seemed cleaner and fresher, and the cars lining the streets were obviously newer and more expensive.

The smell was gone, too, and in its place was a vague scent of gas fumes and flowers. Stopping at one particular corner, I looked down a long, practically endless hill and realized that it was too steep to negotiate comfortably in the declining light, and so I set out in the opposite direction, which led to the top of another hill and a gorgeous view of San Francisco and the bay. I paused momentarily, for the explorer in me couldn't quite believe how beautiful the skyline was when the sky was turning gray and the city lights were beginning to sparkle like diamonds.

There was a small, brightly-lit grocery store shouldered in among some tall buildings, and out of curiosity I crossed the street and sauntered inside. The place was jam-packed with bags and boxes of rice, noodles, and similar foods, and when I finally squeezed my way into the back of the store, I grabbed a generic box of prepared noodles (the perfect food for the way I was feeling) and then began elbowing my way back to the front of the store. Before I reached the register, however, I caught some voices coming from the other side of a tall shelf stuffed with packaged food and gaudy trinkets, and for a second I thought that I had heard my name mentioned. Like anyone else, I stopped for a moment to hear what was being said.

"I don't believe it," one of the voices was saying. It was a woman, and from the pitch of her voice I was certain that she was young, perhaps my age. "Do you mean to tell me she's cheating on him? I find that hard to believe. How do you know?"

There was a slight pause and then a rustling sound as if someone on the other side had just replaced a large box on the other side of the shelf. "Come on, don't tell me you didn't notice it." The voice clearly belonged to a young man, probably the same age as the young woman.

"No, I didn't, because there's nothing to notice. I don't know where you get these ideas from."

"I didn't get these ideas from anywhere. It's obvious. There are certain unmistakable signs..."

"You're kidding, right? There are unmistakable signs of infidelity?" Her voice became a little fainter, and I noticed some slight shuffling sounds which suggested that she was moving toward the front of the store.

"You don't believe there are unmistakable signs of infidelity?" the man responded, his voice now trailing off like hers

Since we all seemed to be headed in the same direction, I turned and began walking toward the register, trying at the same time to keep pace with the couple.

"No, I don't, unless you catch them at it red handed. Are you telling me you caught them red handed?"

"No, of course not..."

"Well, what are they, then? What are the signs that told you they aren't faithful to one another?"

"Not they, just her. She's cheating on him, and I can prove it."

"Really?"

"Yes..."

There was another pause, and I noticed that I was standing in a vague line right beside a young man and a young woman. They were indeed about my age and well dressed, and what surprised me was that they were both looking right at me as though I were intruding into their conversation. Suddenly realizing that I was not actually in line, I smiled at the couple (they didn't respond) and headed back down the aisle to get into line, which now stretched to the back of the store. I, too, wanted to know what those signs were, but since it was fairly obvious that I wasn't going to get close enough to the couple in time to hear the rest of the details, I shoved my noodles into a nearby shelf and squeezed my way out of the store. I tried to spot the couple on my way out, but by the time I reached the door they were gone and I didn't see them outside the store.

Unsettled by this experience (I knew they weren't speaking about me, and yet I couldn't shake the idea that my name had been mentioned), I breathed deeply several times and decided to return home.

I must have been inside the store longer than I knew, for the sun was now gone and, except for the blazing lights emanating from the store and some of the windows in the surrounding buildings, everything was dark and undifferentiated. I crossed the street to retrace my steps, but when I approached the hill that I needed to descend, I became confused. Looking down the long street, which seemed to bottom out in complete darkness, I couldn't locate any of the landmarks I noticed on the way up. Maybe it was the darkness or the fleeting shapes and colors created by blazing headlights reflecting off the buildings as cars came up and over the hill, but I was almost positive that this wasn't my hill – and when I turned back toward the store to get my bearings, I could see the same store on each corner of the intersection. It wasn't a delusion, though; it was nothing more than being in a strange neighborhood at night. With no particular reason to rush, I picked a dark valley and began to trudge downward, certain that somewhere along the way I could catch a cab to go home.

Shaking my head to forget about the strange couple, I had just stepped into the street to hail a cab when I noticed the buildings across the street. The glass façade of the building on my right seemed eerily familiar, and it occurred to me that Luce and I had several discussions regarding the building next to it. It was old, and I remember remarking that the lines and zigzag patterns were characteristic of the art deco period. Naturally, Luce disagreed. "You wouldn't know art deco if it poked you in the eye," she responded, proudly displaying her own ignorance. I turned and there it was right behind me, the apartment building that I knew almost as well as I knew my own building. It was Luce's building, and I had unconsciously strolled across the city to this very place, as if I had purposely… But, no, this wasn't the case. Unlike the other day, I had come here purely by chance.

Staring at her window this time gave me a strange feeling. I can't explain it, but I felt as if I were violating her privacy by being here so late. But that was silly, because I was standing in a public space and had no intention of doing anything without her knowledge. Still, I couldn't shake the feeling, and I dreaded the idea that one of her neighbors should see me and think that I was lurking in the shadows. I immediately turned away from the building and walked to the nearest corner as quickly as I could, hoping to duck out of sight and return home before anyone noticed. I should mention that while I was leaving, I more or less resisted the impulse to take one last look at her window, and yet as I was rounding the corner I could have sworn that one of her curtains moved. My imagination must have been playing tricks on me, for when I did take a quick peek back, the window was dark and the curtains motionless.

I caught a cab about a block away. By the time I walked into my apartment, I felt a little uncomfortable, for I knew that if someone had spotted me near Luce's apartment, he or she might have assumed that I was a peeping tom or a stalker. I am neither, and I reiterated this several times as I turned off the lights and prepared to go to sleep. At the same time, I practically prayed that the slight movement of her curtains was indeed my imagination. If she had seen me, I was certain that it would cause all kinds of problems, especially when I asked about her whereabouts this evening. 'It's a problem, all right,' I remember telling myself just before I fell asleep.

That is, when I fell asleep the first time, because I awoke shortly afterwards and then lay awake for what seemed like hours. I managed to sleep a few minutes later on, but awoke again and couldn't sleep for another hour or so. I didn't know what was causing my restlessness (an excess of caffeine, perhaps), but by the time I had opened my eyes for the last time that evening, the morning light was peeking under my blinds and illuminating half my room. Tired and irritable, I called in sick, despite the clients who were counting on my advice and guidance.

Crawling out of bed around eleven, I went directly into the kitchen to scrounge for something to eat. I had just finished an old hamburger when the phone rang.

"Do you like French food?" asked a sensuous voice on the other end of the line.

"Maybe," I replied cautiously, not immediately recognizing the voice.

"You do or you don't? If you do, then make reservations at Fabre's, and I'll meet you there at 6:00." Before she finished, I recognized Luce's voice and knew immediately that she was following up on her promise to call me.

"Absolutely," I responded, this time with more authority. I was going to suggest that we could travel together, which would be romantic and would eliminate half the fuss of negotiating the city streets and parking, but I didn't have time to say anything else, for as soon as I agreed, she mumbled "don't be late" and hung up. It wasn't a big deal. What mattered was that she followed up on her promise, and I was now hopeful that at the restaurant we might be able to talk about love, which after all was at the root of my anxieties last night.

Chapter 13

When I made the reservation, I insisted on a table in the back. I wanted some place secluded where we could talk without interruption. And the last thing I needed was to be seated in a conspicuous location where someone's gregarious friends might notice and decide to spend the rest of the evening with us.

Reservation aside, I should note that Luce considered herself a knowledgeable Francophile. She often told me how much she appreciated French culture, especially French photographers, and she even claimed to be fluent in the language, which she used now and then to spice up her conversations as if a few foreign words were enough to give her statements greater intellectual weight. But despite this, and despite the fact that we had eaten at any number of restaurants throughout the city, this would be the first time that we set foot in a place that served what was termed "authentic" French food. I was therefore confident that she would be in hog heaven the minute we entered the place, and I was hopeful that it would put her into a receptive mood for what I wanted to say.

Luce was on time for once. Without a word, she presented her cheek for an obligatory peck and then directed the hostess, a young Asian woman, to direct us to our table. We were taken to a quiet place at the back of the establishment directly across from the restrooms. I didn't care. But when the hostess tried to seat Luce, I elbowed her aside and did the honor myself. A few minutes later, the waiter arrived and, after recounting the evening's dinner specials, he asked for our drink orders, speaking pleasantly with a slight French accent. He was an older gentleman, and he wore a soiled, white apron and sported a razor-thin mustache stretching from one corner of his lips to the other. Book and pen in hand, he was about to suggest some wines when Luce interrupted him and inexplicably stated that since it was my birthday, she would be doing all the ordering.

"As it should be, madam," he responded with a slight bow and turned his back to me.

"Please," she added, winking at me. "Speak French, if you understand the tongue."

The waiter smiled, said something in French that I couldn't understand, and again bowed. Holding the drink menu toward the man's face, Luce pointed to something on the right side of the page, which was either overpriced or of questionable value. I mention this only because the choice occasioned a peculiar conversation during which the waiter shook his head once and shrugged his shoulders several times before he acquiesced with a slight and questioning nod. Whatever the issue was, I was determined to dock his tip when the time came.

Later, when the wine-tasting formalities were over (and at least once during this process, I could detect a faint smile beneath the man's bristles when Luce said something about the wine), the waiter pulled his pen and book from his back pocket and was about to say something when Luce interrupted him with brisk wave of her hand.

"Qu'est-ce que c'est les specialities de la maison?" she demanded, seemingly put off by something he was about to say.

"Ce soir, nous avons…," he began, with a weariness now creeping into his voice.

"Non," Luce interrupted, "je ne parle pas de ce soir. Qu'est-ce que c'est les specialities de la maison? Comprenez-vous?"

"Comme vous voyez, notre carte offre les recettes de la vielle France. Une des meilleures est…"

"Ça ne fait rien," she said, again interrupting him with another wave of her hand. "Le plat du jour."

"Ce soir, nous avons un carré d'agneau rôti au miel et au romarin," he started again, but hesitated as if he expected her to say something else at this juncture. When she didn't respond, he slowly began to say what he intended to say – only to be stopped seconds later by another comment that I couldn't in the least bit understand.

I'd never seen anything quite like it. Luce was grilling the poor man with increasing intensity, demanding answers to her questions but interrupting him with additional questions before he had a chance to reply to the earlier questions, which for some reason led her to demand more answers to more questions that she wouldn't let him address. When the interrogation was mercifully over, the waiter retreated to the kitchen to place our orders and Luce leaned back and casually asked me if I had learned anything from the exchange.

"I think I learned that French is utterly incomprehensible, and I wouldn't want to get into a verbal tussle with you if our only language was French," I replied, smiling at my own joke.

Luce failed to find anything funny in what I said, and a cold, cynical glare reminiscent of our time in Carmel quickly came over her face. It didn't last, and moments later the bright, pleasant, and alluring expression that I adored came back. Emboldened by the change, I was about to explain that I wanted to tell her something very special this evening when she frowned and informed me that, once again, I didn't know what I was talking about.

"Let me point out a couple of things," she began and continued rattling on like an angry school teacher. "French is not incomprehensible. It is, on the contrary, a beautiful and expressive language. I'll leave it at that, because it's obvious that nothing I say will make a difference to you. Be aware, though, that what you thought was so incomprehensible was actually rudimentary French. I chose the level purposely. I wanted to see if the waiter truly understood the cuisine and culture that this restaurant, which you picked out, claims to provide."

I didn't point out that she picked out the restaurant, not me. Since I wasn't interested in being on the receiving end of her anger, I merely nodded sympathetically and let her go on.

"It's obvious that he doesn't have a clue about anything," she continued. "Not the language, not the food. He's not only a phony but a fool, and I'm sure the food will be every bit as worthless. There's the wine, I suppose, though it's hardly a suitable vintage."

She eyed her glass briefly and then looked at me, perhaps waiting for me to defend the waiter, the restaurant, or even the wine. Instead of providing more fuel for her fire, I whispered an apology and added sadly that if we left now, it could be hours before we were seated at someplace more suitable. Indeed, I whispered, but not because I was afraid that the waiter would see me groveling before this lovely, petite woman. I was simply trying to keep her under control, and I felt that if I kept my voice and emotions low and calm, she would respond in a similar manner, especially if there were anything else on her mind concerning the staff or the establishment. While she considered my response, I casually glanced around to see if anyone displayed signs of having heard her. Luckily, our waiter didn't seem to be in sight, although I could have sworn that one of the busboys turned away when I looked in his direction. I was afraid that if he heard Luce, he wouldn't hesitate to let with waiter in on what she said, and I didn't want the waiter angry with us before he brought our food.

Luce must have read my concerns on my face, because she smiled sweetly and, glancing down at the table, slowly shook her head as if to say that we were both being a little silly. "Maybe you're right," she whispered back. "His French is passable, albeit in an uneducated way."

The waiter returned a few minutes later, and while he was setting up the table Luce struck up another conversation with him that sounded almost congenial. At one point, he smiled at something she said, although when he turned to me his expression changed, and he appeared dour and world-weary. Brushing it aside as easily as he brushed aside the crumbs on the table, I was beginning to think that we (all of us) had simply started off on the wrong foot and that from that moment on things would be much better. A few seconds later, it occurred to me that as soon as the waiter left I might be able to take Luce's small hand in mine and, looking into her dark eyes, tell her that I loved her and that I couldn't imagine living without her. But once again something intervened to put a hold on what should have been a memorable and magic moment.

When the waiter finished arranging the table, the server appeared with our food and, following the waiter's direction, carefully placed the plates on the table. Once everything was properly distributed, the server disappeared and the waiter, speaking first in French to Luce and then in English to me, inquired if we needed anything else. We smiled, shook our heads, and exclaimed practically at the same time that our food looked and smelled wonderful (that is, I assumed Luce said as much, but I could only go by the pleasant sound of her words). Bowing politely, the waiter motioned with both hands for us to begin eating while he backed away from the table. Luce must have assumed that the man was out of earshot, for it was then that she made a comment in French that stopped him in his tracks (I could see him out the corner of my eye). I don't know what she said, but I could tell by the way he threw his shoulders back and glowered at her that it disturbed him. Suspecting that she again said something offensive, I leaned across the table and told her that I liked the color of the food (I wasn't quick enough to come up with anything better), but she frowned briefly and in English replied that she would say it again if she needed to. "Let's eat already," she added and immediately dug into her dinner.

Despite her initial reservations about the food, Luce attacked her dinner with a gusto that nearly made me sick, and it momentarily quelled any idea I had of making my feelings known to her. Normally, she was a delicate, fastidious eater, and she picked at her food as if she were on a diet or had lost the desire to eat. But this time she devoured everything on her plate, stuffing her mouth full of fish, vegetables, and bread, and then washing it all down with a glass of wine. Once she finished eating every last crumb she could find (excluding those on my plate, which for some reason elicited an expression of disgust when she looked at them) and downed nearly an entire bottle of wine, I half expected her to wipe her mouth with the back of her hand. It may sound as if I'm making too much of this, but I'd never seen this side of her.

The waiter returned shortly afterwards and, bowing pleasantly, handed me the check without looking at Luce. I guess this was the natural thing to do (I was the so-called birthday boy, after all), and yet I couldn't help thinking that he was making a statement of some kind by being friendly to me while ignoring her, which I guess was also natural given her behavior. Later, he took my card and when he came back thanked me and said that he hoped all was well, both with the food and "everything else." I didn't quite know what he meant by 'everything else,' and so I nodded and thanked him for his service. Minutes later as we were heading toward the door, the waiter pulled me aside just after Luce went out the door and whispered in my ear: "You better learn French, my friend, for the woman is very unkind to you."

"What are you talking about?" I demanded, puzzled by his odd words and behavior.

"I am a Frenchman, and therefore I cannot tell you what she said," he replied apologetically. "But I can assure you that it was very unkind."

It occurred to me that he was referring to the comment Luce made while he was standing near the table. While perhaps unfortunate, the comment was hardly as troubling to me as his indiscretion, for he was criticizing the woman I loved, the woman who I hoped might one day… But it didn't matter what I hoped, and so to keep her memory from being sullied after we left, I informed him in no uncertain terms that she was speaking about someone else. He stepped back and, eyeing me, apologized for interrupting. "But," he replied, as if it were an afterthought, "you had better learn French grammar and idioms. Your friend speaks passable French and the word she used, and the context in which she used it, could only refer to you. You are her lover, no?"

I left without replying. Meeting Luce just outside the door, I suddenly felt warm inside because he had referred to me as her lover.

"What took you so long?" she asked as I walked up to her. The night air was cool and brisk, and fetid smells from the street were leeching into the air.

"I was speaking to our waiter," I replied, now wondering what she had actually said.

"Oh, him. I guess you were right. He's not such a fool. Judging by his accent and some of his word choices, I suspect he has a college degree. Sorbonne, perhaps, or the University of Paris, although I can't imagine why someone with such a degree would work in a dump like this."

I looked at her for a moment and then asked her point blank what she said that could have set him off (I mentioned that he was upset about something). "What did you say after the waiter brought our food? You said something and then waved me off when I suggested that we talk more softly."

"What are you talking about? When?"

I repeated my description of the event in greater detail this time, which suddenly brought a look of recognition on her face.

"Oh, that," she chuckled. I expected her to say something about the waiter, and instead she apparently told me the truth. "It was an idiom. In loose translation, I suppose it means something to the effect that my lover is a moron."

I was taken aback by this, of course, because she said it with a straight face. "What?" I asked unbelievingly.

"Oh, don't be paranoid," she replied. "I was talking about my lover."

I didn't know what to say to this. We drove home in silence and, when we arrived at her apartment, she asked me quite pleasantly if I'd like to come in. I begged off, claiming that I had a toothache.

Chapter 14

Should I have been upset by what happened? Sure, her table manners were unappealing, but that's hardly a big deal in the greater scheme of things and, besides, a little love and gentle guidance could work wonders in her case. But what about the rest of it: her rude and insolent behavior toward the waiter and especially her comment about her lover who wasn't me? I didn't expect to see the waiter ever again, but her lover comment was inexcusable, insensitive, disheartening, and all the rest. No, we weren't married, and so having a lover (that is, another lover) was within bounds, I suppose, although it flew in the face of everything that I felt about her and reasonably believed should characterize a close relationship such as ours. If she were telling the truth (and I had no reason to doubt her, although her concept of the truth was sometimes a little difficult to comprehend), then I did the only reasonable thing I could do under the circumstances to keep my sanity and get my life back in order – I severed our relationship. However, I didn't make a clean break (that would have been difficult and maybe even cruel), I just ceased seeing her and stopped responding to her calls and messages, which for a while increased in frequency the longer I remained silent. For a short time, I felt good for having stood up for myself and ended what was, once again, becoming a nightmarish relationship; and yet it didn't take long before reality set in, and I began to miss her and regretted making a decision that had to be made.

Emotional healing may be a function of time (time divided by the square of something and raised to the power of something else, the intangible H), but accepting this did little to improve my mental health, for the pain I felt when making the decision was much less than the pain I experienced one week later, and its intensity didn't relent two weeks after this, or three; the pain only grew over time. Each day was torture – I couldn't sleep, and no matter how hard I tried to find distractions, my thoughts always came back to her and the nagging question of whether or not I had made the right decision. My work didn't suffer, though. If anything, I became more adept during this time at sheltering investments beneath this and that overarching structure, which not only pleased one of the firm's clients but also elicited a begrudging nod from Mr. Rogers, my immediate supervisor. Under different circumstances, I would have been walking on air, but at that moment I couldn't feel anything except leaden and earthbound, and so I went about my work each day because…because I couldn't think of anything else to do. Had I felt the same way in Carmel, I'm not sure I would have been able to leave my room, or if I did, I'm not certain that I could have done any of the things I actually did that week.

However, things took an interesting turn one morning as left my apartment building to go to the office.

I had just rounded the corner of the building when I nearly ran into Luce. One moment I was watching the direction in which my toes were pointing and the next I was standing face to face with Luce, her soft, radiant cheeks and charming smile were encouraging me to embrace her bodily. I refrained, since I couldn't tell if this were an accident or just another stunt designed to humiliate me. Briefly nodding to acknowledge her presence, I tried to step around her, but she mirrored my movements and then laughed at our pantomime as if this were a normal, everyday occurrence.

"Reeky," she finally said, noticeably rolling the 'r.' "I call and send messages, but you don't reply. Please, if I've done anything, let me know. Do you hate me for some reason?"

I stopped without saying a word and turned away. The idea that I should encounter her in front of my apartment (why not in another city or in a large, packed parking lot?) angered me, because this was the one part of the city that I needed to myself, the one part that was key to my solitude and my ability to get on with life without her. It's true that up until this moment I would have given almost anything to speak to her, to hear the soft soothing sounds of her voice as she mangled and re-mangled my name, but at the same time I knew that once I got into a conversation with her, it would be impossible to break away and I could end up in the same downward, humiliating spiral that I was trying so hard to leave and forget. Shrugging my shoulders to signal that our little encounter was over, I stepped to one side and, when she didn't mirror my movement, took another step to go around her.

Sometimes…sometimes, I almost have to question my own sanity, or at least my ability to keep my fingers away from a beautiful but dangerous fire. When she didn't try to block my exit, I hesitated. It was strange that she wasn't putting up more of a fight, especially since she had come all this way for something (and it was obvious that this was no chance encounter). Looking across my left shoulder at her supple figure and drooping head, I noticed a slight tremor in her lower lip and then observed the heavy pools filling her eyes, and for the first time since we met Luce appeared vulnerable; for a moment, she looked like a lost child standing on a street corner. Since the idea that she might actually have a weakness was startling, I couldn't leave things as they were and so I turned to her to explain, calmly and rationally, why getting back together (if that's what she wanted) was a big mistake. Of course, the second I opened my big mouth, I couldn't help saying everything that was on my mind in terms of her inexcusable and possibly deranged behavior.

What startled me even more was that Luce didn't dispute a word of it. She was contrite and agreed with me about everything, noting more than once that she had been a monster (where had I heard this before?) and that she had treated me horribly. But, she noted, it wasn't because she didn't have feelings for me (I would have melted had she used the word 'love'); no, she stressed, it was because she was still traumatized by her nearly fatal accident, and there were moments when she couldn't control her often contrary behavior. Sometimes her head was clear and she lived her new life as promised, but there were other times when things weren't so clear and she reverted to the "mean, old…monster" (she could hardly breathe the word). And, as she quietly and reluctantly admitted, there was another lover. But she dropped him, because he was a fool and she didn't want anything to get into the way of "our" blossoming relationship.

"Reeky, Reeky," she said, snowballing one 'r' after another, "Reeky, you have to believe me. He never meant anything to me. If I truly wanted him, I wouldn't have dropped him. And I dropped him as soon as I understood how much it hurt you. He's gone, I promise you."

"I want to believe you," I said, looking deeply into her dark eyes, "but…"

"I promise to make it up to you. Tell me what I need to do to regain your trust. I'll do anything."

I tried to look away from her to keep from losing my head, but it was almost impossible. Still, I retained enough of my senses to ask her something I couldn't have asked any other time.

"Okay," I began, biting my lower lip, "tell me: Were you with this lover the day you blew off my picnic?"

"Reeky, please…"

"Tell me," I insisted.

She hesitated. "Yes," she uttered quietly.

I was stunned. I had hoped that she wouldn't have been quite so forthright.

"Okay," I stammered, fearing but compelled to press on with my questions. "Were you with him those nights when you weren't home?"

"Maybe. What nights are you talking about?"

"Never mind. It was only one person, right?"

"Yes, that's correct." She started to move closer to me, but I took a half step back.

"I need to know his name."

"Reeky [again and again the 'r's], you don't need to know that. Isn't it enough that I admitted my sin and promised to be true to you?"

I inhaled deeply and demanded the name.

She looked at me and quickly turned away. Silent, she stared at something in the distance, perhaps something that existed only on the horizon of her mind. I was about to demand the name one last time when I realized what a fool I'd been. She didn't need to tell me the name. I already knew it, and I could see its owner as clearly as she could. What a laugh they must have had at my expense – one pretended to be my lover while the other pranced around acting like my close friend and mentor. Stars began filling my eyes and I gritted my teeth so hard that I thought one might break. When I opened my eyes, she had begun to move away as though the revelation was too great for either of us to bear.

Oh, why did it have to be him? I could have accepted anybody but him. Was his party merely a setup designed to humiliate me? Why did it have to be her? Sure, she was stunning, but she was also the most erratic person I ever met and the odds of her changing were slim at best. And why did it have to be me? What did I do to deserve any of this? Do you want to know something pathetically funny? While she was walking away, I wasn't in the least moved by her luminous hair, her perfectly-formed, symmetrical curves, and all the rest. No, what touched me was the slight wobble in her gait caused by the worn heel of her left shoe.

I reached out and touched the back of her right arm.

"Luce," I stammered, barely holding back the emotions welling inside me. "Luce…no, we can't get back together. No, I can't endure another…"

She turned. Large tears were again falling down her soft cheeks. I started to tell her that we couldn't get back together because I couldn't trust her and that she probably needed a lobotomy because she was so difficult to get along with. That is, I opened my mouth, but before I could utter another word she leaned over and rested her wet cheek against my chest. If anything could have stifled cold, remorseless logic – if anything could have could have stopped Socrates in his tracks – it was this. Looking down at the top of her lovely head, I could feel her sobbing against my chest and, seconds later, see the dark spots her tears made on my shirt, and I couldn't go on – I gave in. I grasped her tightly in my arms and began kissing her on the top of her head and on the sides of her face and, after she managed to extricate her head from my grasp, passionately on the lips. Oh, how I loved her, even this early in the morning when passersby were staring at the strange spectacle we made in the middle of the sidewalk.

Perhaps the only smart thing I did at the time was to refrain from uttering the term "love" to express my feelings for her. Sure, I might have gasped something that sounded similar during our caresses, but it was clearly nothing that Luce took seriously since she didn't respond in kind. For the moment, her contrition was enough for me.

Somehow, I managed to get to work on time. Although the front of my shirt was wrinkled, and there were a few smudges and streaks on it from Luce's lipstick and mascara, none of it mattered because we were a couple once again.

Chapter 15

We started slowly and cautiously this time, neither one of us wanting to make the same mistakes over again. It began with dinner that evening, after which we called each other every two or three evenings and went out together on Friday and Saturday nights. Sunday was downtime, which we spent separately in order to keep our relationship fresh and alive. It was not, however, a day in which we freed ourselves from our unspoken commitment to one another (a commitment which included fidelity); it was simply a day which we could spend by ourselves or with a few good friends, preferably those in which there was no possibility of a love interest.

Luce was a different person. She was more accepting and loving than she had ever been, and even though there were moments when she put up a snit or lapsed into stony silence, they were always short-lived and followed by apologies and kisses, lots of kisses. I should also add that I almost never suspected her of infidelity, and so I rarely had the urge to stake out her apartment or accidently wander by in search of something else. In fact, I could see her fidelity in her dark eyes and in the timbre of her voice whenever I would make a sly joke at my former mentor's expense. Indeed, former, for shortly after Luce and I were once again an item, he unexpectedly jumped ship and landed at a large firm in Seattle as a managing partner. Regardless, there were times when I wanted to offer her my little speech about love and commitment, but I studiously postponed it until some vague point in the future. Call me superstitious, but I didn't want to risk our relationship by prematurely explaining the depth of my emotions. A simple "kiss-kiss" sufficed for the time being.

Things had been going fairly smoothly for several months when she and I got into a rather unfortunate and pointless discussion concerning the proper subject of art. Now, I had always been very careful about bringing up anything that might recall the events in Carmel or her precious camera. Through a kind of unspoken agreement, we acted as if the town was of no interest to us and that if either one of us needed a camera, we weren't interested in an expensive German brand (which I couldn't have returned if I had wanted to, since I tossed it down the trash chute in my building shortly after I ceased taking her calls). We even pretended that photography as a subject of interest was passé (there were more important things in our increasingly dangerous world), which sometimes was a little awkward when we strolled past galleries downtown featuring photographers I felt certain she knew. One day, however, neither one of us could restrain ourselves.

We had been in San Francisco most of the day. We visited the museums and the galleries, strolled through the Wharf and Pier 39, and hit several upscale stores as if we were tourists seeing San Francisco for the first time. But we were in love (or headed in that direction), and it felt new and exciting to see all these familiar places with someone special. I made a dinner reservation for 6:00 at a nice place just off the Wharf, and afterwards we planned to spend the rest of the evening at my apartment (we could even take the trolley part way). Well, this was the idea, and throughout most of the day everything went according to plan. Naturally, there were a couple of minor rough spots. Shortly after lunch, I somehow dropped my keys into the trolley tracks and was nearly hit by a car as I desperately tried to fish them out before the trolley arrived. Luce told me that my expression was "priceless" when I spotted the car coming at me, although her expression was less precious when I suggested that it must have mirrored hers when the semi nearly sideswiped her car. "Only an idiot would make such a comparison," she kindly explained to me, but the strain quickly passed and, by the time we were nearly at the restaurant, we both had enough memories of the day to last for years.

Since we still had a few minutes to kill before our reservation, we strolled through Ghirardelli's, looking at the shops and sampling the chocolate. We had reached the end of the shops and galleries when I bent over to tie my shoe. When I stood up, my back facing the shops, I noticed that Luce was staring at something over my left shoulder. Instinctively, I turned to see what it was and noticed a gallery exhibition of photographs – not normal photographs, mind you, but artistic ones, stark x-ray-like images of prisoners sitting in electric chairs, partisans standing in front of firing squads, and gas chambers doing what they do best. At first, I couldn't decipher the images – they appeared to be garish abstractions. But as I examined them more carefully, I could see that they weren't abstractions but images of real people in real situations. I don't have a squeamish disposition, and yet when I finally grasped the import of these images, I let out an involuntary "disgusting" and turned to Luce, expecting the same from her.

Without taking her eyes off the display, she said, "Don't be a fool. This is great art."

I glanced at the images again and met her dark, transfixed eyes. "Who'd want to put that crap on their walls?" I shouldn't have expressed myself this way, but it was a gut reaction to something too visceral for everyday sensibilities.

Luce silently returned my gaze, and for a few seconds I was certain that she was going to badmouth my taste. Instead, she returned to the images and, while concentrating on them, asked me where her camera was. Since this was something totally unexpected, I was at a loss for words.

"It's time to eat," I managed to say but in a rather pathetic voice. "We should probably hurry so they don't give away our reservations. You wouldn't believe how difficult it was to get them…"

Luce turned and glowered at me. "Reeky," she said slowly and deliberately (this time without a rolled "r"), "where is my camera?"

Now, I am a firm believer that truth is always the best policy, even if that truth is unpleasant. In this instance, though, I could see a valid exception to the rule. "What camera?" I asked innocently.

"Don't play games with me. I gave it to you for safekeeping. Now, where is it?"

Luce is a slight person, but the way she planted herself in front of me made her seem bigger than normal and pretty much unmovable.

"Wait a minute," I replied, sensing an opportunity to eliminate one of the dark clouds hanging over our relationship. "What camera did you give me for safe keeping?"

"Are you an idiot? I'm talking about the camera I had in Carmel."

I paused while she searched my soul with her eyes. "Okay, but what is this about you having given it to me for safekeeping? You left it in the room and didn't say a word about it."

"I didn't just leave it there. I left it on the bed for you to protect."

"What? How was I supposed to know that? If you recall, you were furious with me, and I can't believe that in your emotional state you would have left anything for me to keep safely."

She paused and continued to examine me. "Use your head for once in your life. Why would anyone leave a valuable camera behind if it wasn't for someone to protect?

"Because I touched it?"

"Don't be cute. Do you know how much that camera is worth?"

I didn't want to get into a discussion about the cost of the camera, especially because we were attracting a small crowd apparently concerned about the camera. "No, and this isn't the place to discuss it. I'm sure once we've had a little food…"

"No," she replied, acting as if she were speaking to a wayward child. "We are going to discuss it now."

I smiled vaguely, trying to make our discussion seem friendly and even a little amusing to the people crowding around us, but Luce refused to let the matter drop.

"The camera," she insisted. "What have you done with the camera?"

"Please," I tried one more time, pretending to laugh it off as if it were a big joke.

"What's so funny?"

"Okay, okay, I have the camera. Is that what you wanted to hear?" I knew I was in trouble as soon as the words escaped my lips. I would either have to replace the camera or be accused of I don't know what.

Sighing, Luce shook her head as if she had known it all alone. "Well?"

"Well what?"

"Don't play dumb. I want it back."

"All right, I'll give it back. Now, can we go and have some dinner?"

"When?"

"Now."

"You have it with you?"

"Have what with me?"

I could tell that she was gritting her teeth. "The camera, you ignoramus."

"No, no, I put it someplace safe, just like you asked."

"Okay, when?"

"When what?"

"Stop this childish crap," she practically hollered. I wasn't purposely trying to get on her bad side, but it seemed that no matter what I said it was the wrong thing. "When are you going to give it back?"

"Soon. This week, okay?" Once again, I boxed myself in because of the expectations of the crowd.

That mollified her a little, and I gingerly touched her arm and coaxed her toward the restaurant. A handful of people hoping for some more fireworks followed us for about a block, but they were gone by the time we reached the restaurant and took our seats – in complete silence. But Luce didn't seem as pleased as I might have expected given the circumstances. Something was on her mind, something possibly related to the camera, but she didn't say a word for the first thirty minutes or so except to place her order, which she delivered in impeccable English.

She was quiet, all right, but at least she ate like a civilized human being. She didn't stuff her mouth, she chewed with her mouth closed, and she used her napkin and utensils as if she had undergone extensive manners training over the past couple of months. By the time the main course arrived, I had resigned myself to having a silent dinner with a beautiful companion, which I couldn't keep my eyes off no matter how much that camera weighed on us. Mid-way through our meal, though, I began to sense that the other patrons were staring at us, and so I decided to try one more time to elicit something, anything, out of her. Before I said a word, Luce said something in a tone that I had fallen in love with.

"I'm sorry about the camera," she said and smiled, her eyes asking for forgiveness. Unexpectedly, there was a glimmer of hope that I might still slip out of this camera fiasco and maybe even enjoy a pleasant evening with her at my apartment. She didn't even hint that our evening plans needed to be changed.

"Please, don't," I foolishly blurted out. "I understand about the camera. It's very expensive, and I'm sorry it's caused…"

"I'm sure you are, but it's not about the cost. It's more than that."

"It was new, right?"

"Sort of, but that's not the point. There are special memories attached to it. I don't want to bore you with the details here." Once again, Luce became silent, this time staring at her plate as if she were reliving some of those memories.

Naturally, I didn't want to spend the entire evening contemplating our plates or observing some point in inner space, and so I decided to take advantage of her apparent serenity and get a conversation going. But instead of using my head and changing the subject (I didn't want her to start demanding that damned camera again), I tried to get her talking about those memories, which I felt certain were connected to some dotty, drooling old uncle who in his misty youth had once taken a photograph.

"What kind of memories?" I asked innocently.

Looking over my shoulder at something in the distance, she smiled wanly and mentioned that the camera had been a gift from a very special friend.

"Really?"

"Oh, yes," she continued and, without looking at me, revealed that the camera was a gift from my good old buddy in Seattle. I was stunned. I didn't know what to say, especially when she smiled and lovingly uttered the syllables of his name. Shortly afterwards, she sighed and smiled at me, a signal I suppose that her fond memory was over and that she was now ready to focus on reality.

I returned her smile with a stony stare, which she apparently didn't notice. She apparently didn't notice my silence, either, which lasted throughout the rest of the meal and our drive to my place.

Chapter 16

Back at my apartment, on home ground, as it were, I began to feel better and more sociable. So what if that clown had given her the camera? He was long gone, and it was completely normal for her to retain some positive memories of a past friendship. I still had a few fond memories of other women, and I even had a couple of good recollections of my days in Carmel. Well, I quickly put the camera business aside, since Luce appeared to have done the same – she was chatting pleasantly about trifles while mixing drinks and when she sat down on the couch, drink in hand, she promised to make herself a little more comfortable in a few minutes. Using that as my cue, I excused myself to go to the bathroom "to freshen up." I felt a little stupid after saying that, because I was certain that our friend in Seattle never needed freshening.

Luce smiled alluringly as I got up. I could feel her dark eyes on me as I strolled to the bathroom, skipping past my desk which was next to the bathroom door, and quietly closed the door behind me. Leaning over the sink, I splashed warm water over my rough face (I hadn't shaved in a couple days), tidied up my thick eyebrows (smoothing some of the errant hairs with a moistened thumb) and breathed a little more easily that the camera was no longer front and center. Of course, should the subject again rear its ugly head, I was prepared to buy another camera regardless of cost if that's what it took to make the whole ugly affair go away. After checking the status of my deodorant, I dabbed some cologne on my chest and fluffed up my hair. Just as I was ready to return to the most beautiful woman in the world, I noticed several faint whooshing sounds outside of the door. Pressing my ear to the door, I detected some indecipherable moans or groans that were immediately followed by the unmistakable echoes of drawers being slammed shut. None of this made any sense unless Luce was watching one of her lame TV shows.

Full of pleasant expectations, I opened the door and found Luce grasping something with one hand and slamming one of my desk drawers closed with the other.

"What's going on?" I asked, not quite believing my eyes. I couldn't understand what she was doing, and I would never have suspected her of trying to steal anything.

She glanced angrily at me and then opened one more drawer, which happened to be empty, and slammed it shut.

"Where is it?" she demanded, as if I were subject to her commands.

"Where is what?"

Luce bared her teeth, and for a moment I couldn't help thinking that she might actually attack me. Breathing deeply, as though her anger unexpectedly left her short of breath, she demanded her camera back.

"What?"

"Don't what me, you stup…you said the camera was here in a safe place. It's my camera, and I want it back…now!"

I stepped closer to her, but stopped when her body became rigid. "I didn't say I had it here," I replied, desperately trying to come up with something to justify its absence. "I…I said it's in a safe place."

She glowered silently for a moment. "All right," she replied, calling my bluff, "let's go get it. I want it back tonight."

Looking at Luce, observing her narrow eyes and the way in which she slowly opened and closed one of her small fists, I was suddenly reminded of that idiot friend of hers, the one who photographed man-eating bugs (or was it the death chambers?), and I couldn't help thinking that she was ready to consume me at the slightest verbal slip. Luckily, the response that came to mind was the only thing short of delivering the camera that could have pacified her. "It's in my safety-deposit box," I lied. "I can't get to it tonight." I suppose it was a stupid thing to say, since it only deferred the inevitable for another day, but I loathed the idea of sitting

80

through another storm (one, I should add, that would not inhibited by casual onlookers) and, besides, there was always a chance that something would come up to push the inevitable even farther into the future. Nevertheless, I braced for the worst…and for some reason the worst didn't happen. Luce became silent, her posture relaxed, her hands dropped to her sides, and the withering expression that hardened her face softened, leaving her as sweet and beautiful as she always was. It was over and, with the camera an issue for another day, I was certain that we could savor the evening as planned.

The change was mesmerizing, especially when she lowered her eyelids, which made her look like one of Correggio's gentle Madonnas. Seizing the moment, I gently grasped her arm and cautiously led her back to the couch, where I helped her down onto its thick cushions. I sat down next to her and, holding my breath as if I could be making a mistake, wrapped my arm around her shoulders while she snuggled next to me.

Of course, this was hardly the first time we pressed our clothed bodies together. But after a few quiet minutes, something seemed different about the situation. Perhaps it was merely the relief we felt at ending something that could have become much worse, or maybe it was simply the settling of the chemical processes that had been aroused by the camera. It may have been something else entirely, for I felt a warm sensation welling inside me that had nothing to do with sex (or very little to do with it), and I wanted to tell her that I loved her. At the same time, I hadn't quite reached the point at which I could easily lower my defenses and expose my heart. It didn't help matters that the overhead lights were still on and casting a clinical glare throughout the room, and to eliminate this impediment to any expression of love and intimacy would require untangling ourselves, after which I would have to walk across the room to flip the switch, which would have broken the spell if not a toe or two when I had to grope my way back to the couch in complete darkness.

I decided to leave well enough alone, for Luce changed her position slightly and pressed her body closer to mine. I thought about reaching for her face and lips, but she began slowly caressing the top of my right leg with the tip of her middle finger. For a few moments, she made soft, clockwise circles on my neatly-pressed kakis and then, reversing direction, she inscribed even smaller circles on the same spot in a counterclockwise direction. This continued for a few more moments until for some reason, she stopped, smoothed out the wrinkles in pants with a single crisscross stroke. It was magic, and I closed my eyes and pressed my chest against her shoulders to intensify the sensation. She moved slightly, I may have been putting too much weight against her shoulders, and a second later I leaped off the couch and practically knocked Luce to the floor.

Holding my leg while dancing a jig, I felt a small, coin-like object on the top of my pants and, looking down, spotted the shiny, metallic head of a thumbtack centered on the very spot that Luce lovingly stroked. She was now sitting upright on the couch, arms crossed, with a snarl having replaced her beatific smile.

"What, what, what?" I practically shouted, not quite comprehending what had happened. "What did you do that for?"

"I did it to teach you a lesson." She relaxed somewhat and the snarl changed to disdain.

"Lesson? Are you out of your mind?"

"Don't be such a baby," she replied calmly, as if she were speaking to a child who had just stepped on a small, insignificant thorn.

"Baby? Ouch…"

"Oh, come here, you knucklehead. I'll help you." She leaned forward and, like the hapless mate of a black-widow spider, I limped over and presented my leg.

The thumbtack's silvery head was still visible albeit smudged with streaks of red blood, while around its edge a dark circle about the size of a quarter was expanding on my pants and would soon exceed the diameter of a dollar. If there was anything funny about the incident, it had to be the tack itself, for it was the

82

very tack I used to stick the picture taken of us in Carmel to the wall above my desk (before tossing the camera, I downloaded the picture and printed it). Could Luce have noticed the picture when she pulled the tack from the wall?

Unable to turn away, I watched Luce calmly pluck the thumbtack from my quivering leg, using her thumb and the polished nail of her forefinger. I probably yelped, because my ears were ringing and I noticed that she…smiled. No, that couldn't have been right. Even Luce wasn't that cruel, although she examined the weapon between her fingers for a couple of seconds before tossing it over her shoulder and then wiping her bloody fingers onto my tan couch.

Like a deer caught in the headlights, I mindless watched everything around me as if these things were happening to someone else, that is, until she pulled me onto the couch next to her. Oddly, I remember wondering if she pulled me down onto the blood spot. At any rate, she immediately leaned toward me and whispered in my left ear, "Next time, think twice before being so cavalier with other people's property."

"What are you talking about?" I managed to sputter but was immediately silenced when she placed her index finger softly against my lips.

"You know what I'm talking about. But it's over. You can have the camera, and we'll pretend this moment never happened – we'll pretend the camera never existed. One thing, however – I don't want to see it ever again."

"But, but, I swear…," I began but stopped. Luce was eyeing me as if I were going to tell a whopper, and so I dropped the subject. The camera had finally been put to rest, and I had the good sense to recognize that one more word and it could have come raging back to life.

Chapter 17

I still can't believe how smoothly the rest of the evening went. After Luce helped me remove my bloody pants (I'm sure I grimaced once or twice as she yanked the fabric away from the quickly congealing blood), she cleaned the wound with a paper napkin, dabbed some petroleum jelly on it, and slapped a tiny, circular bandage on it. Sometimes, I wonder if she could have had some training as a nurse or caregiver (she never disclosed her educational background), and even when she chided me for being a "baby," adding that I was an idiot for putting up such a fuss, I sensed something concerned, thoughtful in her ministrations – she seemed to enjoy tending to my wound even more than she did causing it. Well, this was the worst of it, and soon as I was put back together, Luce became lovely and charming again, and we snuggled together on the couch for a few hours, watching TV. I woke up the following morning thanking my lucky stars that she was lying next to me and that the swelling on my leg didn't appear to portend a more serious injury. I was also thankful that the stinking camera was finally a thing of the past.

We went our separate ways during the day, but we met later for dinner and again repaired to my apartment. This evening was every bit as nice as the previous one, more so because I had no occasion to cry out in pain, and she not only stayed the night but the following day and night as well. In less than a week, Luce was practically living at my apartment, even on Sunday.

Given this, it might be surprising to hear that we never discussed making the arrangement a bit more permanent. I have no doubt that Luce would have agreed, but at the time it seemed a little too soon in our relationship to take such a big step. In the first place, I hadn't made a formal declaration of my love, and it didn't make sense to live with someone without making the kind of commitment that a declaration of that type implies. Bumping shoulders in the kitchen, sharing the bathroom and its fixtures, treating the entire apartment itself as if what's mine was hers, not to mention ceding our personal and private spaces on a day-to-day basis – no, that was too much for me without coming to the sort of mutual understanding that a declaration of that kind necessarily implies. And in the second place…well, the second place was pretty much a reiteration of the first, but with the question of whether the feelings we shared were deep enough to take the next step. Did I truly love her? Yes, and I was increasingly certain that my feelings were as profound as love could be. But did she love me? I wasn't quite as sure about this, even though the way she looked and touched me suggested something deeper than normal friendship – and I simply wasn't ready to risk everything without at least a tacit assurance that my declaration would be reciprocated.

For the time being, I didn't dwell too much on the semantics of love. I tried to be content with its physical manifestation and the occasional "luv ya" or "smooches" concluding this or that. Interestingly, when we were together, we either spent the night at my apartment or at a hotel, never at Luce's apartment. For some reason, Luce never wanted to stay at her place unless she was there alone. She had a perfectly respectable apartment, but she always deferred bringing me there because it needed to be cleaned, or it was too small, or the bed was uncomfortable, or the neighbors were noisy, or it was something else. And she refused to move to a different apartment, because it was either too expensive or too much trouble or too something else, and so as I said we spent most of our evenings either at my place or at a hotel (when I had the money to splurge). Don't get me wrong, we usually had a good time at hotels, but I would have preferred my apartment or even hers, with its barking neighbors and noisy dogs.

One evening about a month after the thumbtack incident, we spent an evening at the San Francisco Maypole, an upscale, traditional-style hotel noted for hosting presidents and heads of state. It was my idea, because we were spending the day in the city, and it just seemed like the romantic thing to do. That morning, we launched off from my apartment to the zoo, after which we spent the rest of the afternoon at Fisherman's Wharf. Later on, we ate (splurged!) at one of the hotel's restaurants; by that time we were completely exhausted and thankful for a quiet table at the very center of the establishment. Luce was a wonderful companion throughout the day, and, by the time we finished dinner that evening, we could hardly drag both ourselves and our packages up to our room, where we collapsed on the bed, barely able to turn on the TV. It was only eight o'clock, and yet we practically fell asleep in one another's arms. Actually, I dozed off and was awoken at ten when Luce asked me to accompany her for a quick stroll through the hallways.

"Why," I asked, not completely clearheaded. "Can't we do that in the morning?"

"No, silly. I love walking through the hallways at good hotels, and I want to do it now. Later on, we can walk over to the Grand [another noted hotel a couple blocks away] to ride the elevator. In case you haven't noticed, it's almost entirely glass and it runs on the outside of the building. You can see most of the city from it. There's also a wonderful rooftop garden with great views."

How could I refuse? She looked so sweet and innocent, and it was almost impossible to believe that this was the same individual who had gone into hysterics over a stupid camera. Within minutes, we were quietly strolling through the hallways eyeing this and that, and shortly afterwards walking down the dark, glittering streets toward the Grand. Fifteen minutes after leaving the hotel, we were sailing up the half-invisible elevator toward to the building's rooftop terrace. While I wasn't keen on going out so late, I have to admit that the glittering city views from the elevator and especially the terrace were spectacular, especially when Luce propped her elbows on the top of the short wall surrounding the terrace and stared out into the dark, cloudless night. Without a word, I stepped behind her and put my arms around her waist and felt the warmth of her body and smelled the jasmine scent of her hair. Shortly afterwards, Luce turned around in my arms and, looking into my eyes, reached up and pressed her lips against mine. It was a moment that could have been made for a movie.

I continued to hold her closely. I kissed her lips and face, and I rubbed my check against her beautiful and fragrant hair. But it wasn't until I noticed her left ear and observed its delicate color and perfect curvature that I knew the time had come for me to confess my love. Furthermore, as I followed the ear's fluting to the lobe, the lobe itself seemed to assure me that Luce felt the same and was waiting for my confession. Turning toward her face, I looked into Luce's eyes and was about to say something about love when she laughingly wriggled out of my arms and, grabbing my hands, pulled me back toward the elevator. We rode the elevator up and down a good twenty times before we had seen enough of the city and it was time to go back to our hotel. Strolling back along the dark streets, we silently held hands and from time to time smiled at each other or at something unseen in the night. Naturally, I was disappointed that I hadn't told her what was in my heart, but I was confident that once we were again in our room, the opportunity would be there to say everything that needed to be said. By the time we reached the room, I was ready and even had a couple of phrases prepared that would help launch me into the whole business. But when we entered the room, Luce headed immediately to the bar and fifteen minutes later was curled up in the bed and snoring contentedly.

Even if I didn't say the words, the evening itself was wonderful, and I was convinced that a foundation was being laid for my confession. Since we couldn't replicate this moment in time, I took a chance a couple of days later to suggest that we drive to Lake Tahoe for the weekend. Luce accepted my proposal without hesitation.

Now, I hadn't forgotten our trip to Carmel and all the trouble that reverberated throughout our relationship for some time afterwards (and maybe still did, since neither one of us spoke about the camera, even casually), but I was fairly certain that this trip would be different because, unlike the first, we knew each other much better and we had already experienced the trials and tribulations of a relationship. We were also much closer, especially after the night at the Maypole, and we had shown that we could spend more than a few hours together without getting in over our heads. Finally, we didn't have to deal with that accursed camera. But just to be on the safe side, I had arranged for a weekend trip, knowing full well that the unexpected could always rear its ugly head at the least provocation.

Chapter 18

Lake Tahoe lies in the Sierra Nevadas about five hours by car from San Francisco. The lake is one of the deepest in the world, and from shore to shore it is well over twenty miles. Surrounded by deep pine forests and nestled in among casinos, hotels, and fine restaurants, the water is bluer than the clearest sky and icy cold.

Unlike our Carmel trip, this afternoon was clear and gloriously warm, filling me with joy and making me confident that the weekend would be special. With my single bag neatly stowed in the corner of my trunk, I arrived at Luce's building shortly after lunch, having left the office early so that we could reach the lake before sunset or, if we were lucky, while the setting sun was casting its golden rays across the shimmering surface of the water. Oh, I could already see us driving along the highway that wound its way through the evergreen forests to the tops of the mountains and, after cresting the last ridge, slowly descending into the valley where the lake glistened in the dying light.

Luce seemed as enthusiastic about the trip as I was (this was her first time to the lake), and, as she informed me a couple of days before our departure, she was taking off the Thursday before the drive to prepare for it (I didn't know what she taking a day off from, since as far as I knew she was still between "positions," or why she needed an entire day to prepare). She talked incessantly about the trip in the days leading up to our departure, and I think she even did some rudimentary research on the lake and the environment surrounding it. But when she finally greeted me at her door (and this after twenty minutes of buzzing her intercom, calling her cell, and buzzing her intercom again, and again), she appeared tired and disorganized; and, despite her perfectly respectable slacks and blouse she was wearing, as well as the white baseball cap she donned with her ponytail sticking out the back, she claimed that she wasn't dressed for such a long drive.

Naturally, I began to think of Carmel, but I didn't say anything and sat patiently on a hard chair for well over two hours while she changed, showered, packed, repacked, and changed again. When she said that she was finally ready, I lugged all five of her oversized bags down the stairs and carefully arranged them in the trunk so that I could close it securely. I made myself comfortable in the driver's seat, but then had to wait another forty-five minutes or so while she went back for something she might have forgotten. Once we were out of the city (and because she had taken so long, we had to negotiate the afternoon rush traffic), she became bright and cheery, chatting about this and that while I kept glancing at her charming profile and bouncing ponytail, and the manner in which her tennis shorts and silk blouse clung to her body. I was in heaven and, because of the way she rattled on, it was reasonable to conclude that she was there, too, or at least in the neighborhood.

Once we were in the mountains, about two hours from the lake, the highway was clear, and we chatted about the beautiful forests, the occasional animals on the side of the road (or on the road itself), and some of the things we wanted do once we got there. Since we were staying at a large hotel/casino next to the lake, we talked about the hotel shows (including one she dismissed as "juvenile" that I secretly hoped we could see), the hotel restaurants, the hotel gift shops and stores, and finally the lake. We both wanted to get our feet wet (the lake is too cold for swimming this time of the year), walk or bicycle along the shore, take a boat ride, and maybe picnic some place in the forest. I suggested having dinner on the old paddlewheel boat that cruised the lake most evenings, and Luce not only jumped at the idea, but she also said that with the moon shining on the water, it would be "positively romantic" – yes, she used these very words. It was long past sunset when we arrived, but the water along the shore of the lake sparkled with colorful, star-like lights.

We immediately checked into our room (already it was different experience than Carmel) and, since neither one of us was particularly hungry (without complications, we had stopped at a little café along the way), we took a nice stroll along the lake. Hand in hand, we walked a few yards, stopped and gazed out at the water, walked another few yards, paused and admired the rainbow of beautiful casino lights reflecting off the lake's surface, and walked some more, kicking up the sand and dirt with our toes and laughing quietly (the solitude and the depth of our feelings for one another kept our volume down). We chatted more about tomorrow's plans and then discussed ideas for this evening's dinner. Since many of the restaurants in the area are open all night, we had a variety to consider before we finally chose the buffet at our hotel. After stuffing ourselves, we strolled through some of the hotel's gift shops and finally went to our room. By this time, we were ready for bed, and we practically fell into each other's arms and slept soundly the rest of the night.

The following morning before we went out, I arranged for a late dinner on the paddleboat, and then throughout the day we drove around the lake, checked out picturesque places at various points along the shore, and tried out a couple of restaurants along the way (one for breakfast, another for lunch). Later that afternoon, we went to the casino but Luce quickly lost the money I had given her on the roulette table, and by that time we were ready for an evening dinner and cruise.

The paddleboat adventure was unquestionably the highlight of the day. We had a nice table in the grand salon – a large, ornate hall that was filled with glimmering chandeliers, white pillars, and elegant tables – near one of the giant windows that opened up to a spectacular view of the now black lake and the boat's lights sparkling on the water. Luce was smiling and chatting throughout the entire event and, at one point, even leaned across the table and told me that she was having a "wonderful time." And it was then, with the words "wonderful time" reverberating in my ears – it was then that I decided to tell her what was in my heart. But, as usual, something intervened to prevent me from expressing my love to her (if it wasn't the waiter, then it was the rowdy diners at the table next to us, and if it wasn't them, then it was something else, always something else). Having had no luck by the time the boat was lumbering back into the dock, I couldn't stand it anymore and blurted out more loudly than I intended that I loved her. I could have fallen face-first in my soup when Luce responded by leaning across the table and kissing me lightly on the cheek, a gesture that was accompanied by the boat's unexpected lurch (Luce fell back into her chair) and the raucous laughter and smooching sounds from the rowdies at the table next to us. It didn't matter, for I was in heaven – Luce not only accepted my declaration, but she reciprocated with a kiss and…did she say the word "love"? I don't recall.

The next day was just as wonderful. We saw the lake again, ate in a couple different restaurants, and visited several gift shops in our hotel and along the main street. It was almost evening by the time we were on the road again, and from that moment until we actually reached San Francisco, we chattered like high school sweethearts. Luce brought back a large bag of souvenirs (clothing and trinkets from the shops, including a trashy picture of the lake with the casino's neon sign obscuring half of it, as well as some pine cones and other debris from the beach), while I had memories that I recorded without a camera. Interestingly, while we were passing through Sacramento, Luce quietly opened up about her family. She mentioned her eccentric but "brilliant" father, who disappeared one afternoon in the New York subway system thirty years ago, her equally "brilliant" but slightly unbalanced mother, who retired to Arizona after declaring that the bottoms of the waiters there were much better than those in New York, and her beautiful sister, who lived somewhere in the Bay Area. She was younger than Luce and both "brilliant" (naturally) and emotionally unstable (unsurprisingly).

Since it was late in the evening as we approached the city, I asked Luce if she would like to spend the night. My apartment was closer, I reasoned, and it wouldn't be any trouble to take her things to her apartment in the morning on my way to the office. She agreed, and fell asleep shortly before we arrived at my place.

I practically carried Luce to my apartment. She was tired and her feet hurt, and she told me in a sleepy voice that she didn't think she could make it up the stairs without some help. After she was settled in, I went back to the car, at her insistence, and hauled up all her increasingly heavy bags. Naturally, I was initially reluctant to waste all this time and effort when I would only have to haul them all down in the morning, but as I considered the matter more I realized that once her things were neatly tucked away in my apartment, I might be able to coax her into staying the rest of the week, maybe longer. And, if things went as well as I hoped, we could be ready to begin serious negotiations on setting up housekeeping together. I loved Luce, and she loved me, and housekeeping was the next reasonable step in a relationship that was bound by love and loyalty.

By the time I was done, my own legs ached and I was so tired that I was barely able to crawl into bed next to her. But as it turned out, this was one of the most wonderful nights of my life. Nothing happened, we were too tired, and when I heard Luce snoring quietly next to me, I realized that this was the kind of mundane experience that lies at the heart of real love – for real love, the kind of love that endures hardships and lasts a lifetime, is born from the shoulder-to-shoulder, hip-to-hip trust and companionship that makes the mundane experiences of living and dying meaningful. I woke up long before the sun rose and, seeing and feeling Luce cuddled up next to me, tried to wait out the rest of the night until she awoke and I could tell her this, hinting at a more permanent living arrangement between us.

I didn't last until sunrise. When I finally opened my eyes, the sun was streaming through my window, forcing me to shield them with my right forearm. With my left hand, I reached over to Luce only to find a vacant space next to me. I sat up, scratched my right shoulder, stretched my neck, and then strolled into the living room just in time to see the front door close and to hear a succession of mouse-like squeaks accompanying her suitcase as she pulled it down the hallway toward the elevator. Dashing first to the window, I spotted a cab directly below, its engine running and its trunk open, and the driver trying to coax one of her suitcases into the trunk. I charged back to the door and by the time I was standing in the hallway, I witnessed the last corner of her suitcase roll into the elevator and then the doors closing with a muffled thud.

"Luce," I called out, running pointlessly toward the elevator. I knew I was too late, and yet I couldn't stop pounding on the button several times in a futile effort to arrest the machine's relentless downward progress. I gritted my teeth and shook my head, and yet I remained standing in front of the bronze doors unable to decide if I should wait for the elevator or return to my apartment. One of my neighbors, an elderly woman with yellow hair who never went anywhere without a small, rat-like dog nestled in her arms, came up beside me and asked me if I were going out for a bit. Smiling meanly, her jowls shaking, she seemed to be in on some monstrous joke that completely eluded me. I turned without responding, and it was only after the little rat nipped me that I got the punch line – I was naked except for my underwear. I walked back to my apartment with as much dignity as I could muster and, once safely inside (and I was lucky the door wasn't locked), charged to the window and observed Luce handing her last bag to the angry driver.

I pulled and banged and pushed frantically on the frame, and no matter what I did the window wouldn't budge. Since this was the only window in my apartment facing the street, I started pounding on the glass (careful to avoid shattering it) and hollering Luce's name. "Luce, Luce," I shouted over and over, praying that she could hear me. "Wait, I'll take you home."

Luce hesitated and then glanced around as if she heard something but couldn't tell whether it emanated from someone down the block or from a passing car, which squeaked, banged, and clanged as noisily as a trolley. Shrugging her shoulders, she was about to get into the cab when something, maybe my voice, made her stop and look up toward my window, where I continued pounding and hollering desperately. While I had her attention, I tried to tell her to wait, I tried to tell her that I would be down momentarily, using words and a variety of hand signals, but she didn't seem to understand a word or signal of what I was trying to convey to her. She shook her head and, without so much as a smile or wave, started to get into the vehicle.

I needed to stop her, if only momentarily. I needed to find out why she was leaving so abruptly. I needed to arrest her movement before she walked out of my life like she tried to do in Carmel, if indeed this was what she was doing. But I didn't know what to do. I couldn't run after her, there wasn't enough time, and even if I managed to reach the cab, what could I do to stop its motion – jump in front of it (far too dangerous in this town)? Desperate, I tugged at the window with all my strength, and this time it shot up to the top of the frame where it stopped with a loud crack. Not wasting a second, I stuck my head out and hollered the first thing that came to mind. "Luce," I cried as she was pulling her leg into the car. "Luce, I love you. Marry me."

I think there was a moment of hesitation – her leg stopped midair before retreating into the cab – but I'm not sure. The door closed and seconds later the car sped off.

I remained leaning out the window for several minutes in case she returned with an answer to my proposal. When it was obvious that she wasn't coming back, I slowly retracted my head and closed the window (or tried to, since now it wouldn't go down all the way). Had she heard me and, instead of granting a formal reply, departed with the tacit understanding that such a relationship could never be? Was this the end of our relationship, with or without marriage? Had I humiliated myself by asking a premature and completely inappropriate question? These and a thousand variations of the same thing floated through my mind, and at least for the time being I had no answers. Since she was difficult to reach in the morning, I deferred calling until later and instead went to the office, where I could keep my mind intact by concentrating on other things.

Not surprisingly, that day was one of the longest in my life. I tried to call Luce several times but she didn't pick up and her message service wasn't working. Was she refusing to answer me? In between the calls, I tried to do a little work, but

95

the numbers either floated across the screen or hid themselves in irrelevant folders, and so it was almost impossible to complete the simplest of tasks. Sometime after lunch I realized that Luce might be legitimately busy (why not?), and so I resolved to wait until the evening before trying her again. When I returned home, I checked my phone and email messages, and there was nothing except advertisements and a smarmy note from a politician telling me that he was certain that I agreed with him about something. Collapsing onto my now empty couch, I tried to figure out when I could reach her, assuming of course that she would take my call. After fifteen minutes or so of fruitless contemplation, interspersed with the fear that I had lost the love of my life, the phone rang. It was Luce, and she wanted to know if I were interested in watching TV with her this evening. Naturally, I jumped at the opportunity, and she promised to come right over.

While I truly didn't have a free evening (I had a vague recollection that my briefcase was full of papers that were due the first thing in the morning), I needed to know if Luce had heard me and, if so, if she would consent to be my lawful wife.

Chapter 19

I anticipated Luce's arrival within minutes of our short conversation. I knew it was unrealistic to expect her so soon – even if she lived across the hall, it could easily take her a good forty-five minutes to reach my front door, given her feeble grasp of time and her limited respect for punctuality – and yet during the first hour after our conversation, I couldn't help running to the door every thirty seconds or jumping up every time I heard a creak, groan, or bump in the hallway. During the second hour, instead of nervously bouncing around, I remained seated and obsessed over whether she had been in an accident or had changed her mind about coming over. I called her several times, but there was no answer, and there was no response to my text inquiries, which fueled my anxiety and filled my head with all sorts of horrific images. Once or twice, I tried to imagine how I would nurse her back to health after some terrible accident, but each time I bent over to kiss her moist forehead, she turned away and in a delirious fever called out for John or Phil or someone else to save her. Luce's arrival nearly three hours later mercifully put an end to these particular nightmares. Waltzing through the door as if nothing unusual had happened, she offered neither an apology nor an excuse for being late.

I didn't say anything about the time (it was nearly ten). Really, it didn't matter, because I was happy to see her safe and sound in my apartment, and I was tickled that she was apparently glad to see me, even if she hadn't thought twice about worrying me over her delay.

"I'm glad I caught you," she said as she sat down on the couch, kicking off her shoes and tucking her legs under the thin sun dress she was wearing. Grabbing the remote, which was on the coffee table next to the couch, she switched on the TV, selected a channel, and lapsed into a dull silence while she stared intently at a bunch of talking heads spouting the same mindless party line.

I sat down next to her, pretending to be interested in the show, but when I tried to scoot closer to her, she moved away as if she needed extra space to concentrate. We sat silently for several minutes, nodding sagely while some mental lightweight piously uttered the same vacuous drivel that every other mental lightweight had been uttering for several weeks, but when a screaming commercial complemented the dignity of the foregoing show, I took the opportunity to make some small talk.

"Traffic bad?" I offered, trying to sound sympathetic.

"What?" she asked, without taking her eyes off the set.

"Was the traffic bad? I thought you'd be here earlier."

She glanced briefly at me, her expression perplexed and uncomprehending, and then turned back to the TV, which was now airing a commercial about a surgical procedure guaranteed to bring the life back into zest, or something like that. Observing a slight frown on her lips and noticing that she adjusted her legs a little, I naturally assumed that this would be a good time to get a conversation moving. I repeated my question, but instead of weighing in she merely glanced at me and muttered, "Yeah, sure."

Since the talking heads were back on the air, I turned back to the set and tried to understand what was so fascinating about their predictable proclamations, but after a few minutes I couldn't stand listing to them and had to find out if she had heard me yesterday as she was leaving. Of course, I knew that I risked causing a row by interrupting her concentration, but at the moment I was willing to take that risk, and I hoped that if her answer was affirmative, she wouldn't mind the interruption.

"Luce," I began cautiously, tapping her lightly on the arm. "Can we talk for just a couple minutes?"

Luce didn't respond and instead narrowed her eyes as if she were trying to concentrate on what one of those airheads was saying. I repeated her name and gave her another soft touch on the forearm, which was enough to elicit a slight grimace but not pull her eyes from the screen. Finally, sensing that I was looking at her, she muttered, "What? Sure, but does it have to be right now? I wanted to see this, and my set's on the fritz." She trailed off as if nothing else needed to be said.

Had she wanted to come over merely because her set was on the fritz? "This is important," I insisted.

Again, she didn't look at me. "What?"

"Are you listening to me?"

She turned to me briefly and then returned to the set. "Can't it wait until after the show? Didn't I tell you that my TV's broken?"

I was silent for a few minutes while I puzzled over what to do. At last, when the next set of commercials started blaring, I gathered my courage and said, "This is important."

Luce turned her head toward me, a cold expression marring her otherwise beautiful features. Even then, she wasn't giving me her full attention, for every now and then her eyes would dart back to something on the screen.

I pressed on, suspecting that I only had a few seconds to say what I needed to say. "Did you hear what I asked you yesterday morning?"

"What?" she replied, acting like I was uttering nonsense.

"Yesterday, I asked you something. Actually, I asked you something when you were leaving the building for your cab – and I really don't know why you couldn't wait for me to drive you. It wasn't a problem. I was happy to do it."

"What are you babbling about?" she demanded, scrunching up her eyes at me and then turning back to the TV.

I hesitated, knowing that if I upset her, a simple yes could turn into a resounding no. "Luce, please try to concentrate on what I'm saying."

"I am, but you're not making any sense. I took a cab, because I called for a cab. Why are you giving me the third-degree?"

"No, no," I said, and gently picked up her limp hand. She was concentrating on another commercial and evidently didn't notice that I held her hand in mine. "That's okay. What I mean is…well, did you hear what I said as you left my building?" I hesitated for a moment, my heart now pounding in my chest. "I told you I loved you, and I said something else. Did you hear that?"

"Which?" she mumbled, still focused on the TV.

I couldn't stand it anymore. I needed to know, and I needed to know now. "Did you hear me asking you to marry me?"

She said something I couldn't understand.

"What? I asked you to marry me."

She didn't respond and seemed mesmerized by a novel depilatory, razor, or something like that. Feeling as though I were fighting a losing battle, I was ready to turn off the TV and toss the remote out the window when she glanced at me and said, "Yes, I heard you."

For a second, I was thrilled – she had heard me and her answer was yes – but then as I quickly mulled it over, I realized that she hadn't said yes or no. In fact, I wasn't even sure that she was responding to something I had said.

"Luce, for God's sake, listen to me. Can you turn that stupid thing off for at least one minute?"

Her jaw tensed, and she histrionically forced down the mute button on the remote. "I can hear you," she said angrily, now turning her full attention to me.

"Please…I'm sorry, I guess this isn't the time." All of a sudden, I wasn't so certain that I wanted to know the answer.

"I'm all ears, Reeky," she replied, violently rolling the 'r.' "Can you be quick about it?"

"All right," I said, beginning to get a little angry myself. "All right, I want to know if you heard me yesterday asking to marry you?"

She looked at me as if I were crazy. "Yes, I heard you. Is that why you interrupted my show?" She turned back to the show and clicked the sound on.

"No…I mean, yes. What's your answer?"

"To what?"

"To my proposal." I was beginning to get heated, especially because she seemed to be more engaged by what some pudgy-faced jackass was jabbering about than what I asked her.

"Can't we discuss this after the...what did he say? You made me talk right through his answer."

I stood up. I knew I needed to remain calm, but the way she was acting...infuriated me. "What about my answer?" I shouted.

"I can't believe it," she said, shaking her head. "It's over. I don't know why I had to come here for this nonsense." She shut off the TV and turned to me, staring fiercely.

So it was over, I told myself. Had I remained a little calmer, perhaps she might have had a different answer. I felt like kicking myself for demanding an answer that could have waited a few more minutes, maybe even another day. I shook my own head and plopped back down on the couch, fully expecting Luce to jump up and leave...forever.

"Are you okay?" she asked, her features softening.

I nodded vaguely, silently. I could hardly move under the weight of my disappointment and stupidity.

"Okay, so what was so important that you had to interrupt my show?"

I looked at her, and I could tell from her now charming eyes and pleasant smile that her refusal hadn't been directed at me but at the blathering idiots on TV. I hesitated. "Did you...did you understand what I had asked you yesterday?"

Luce looked at me as if I had said something that was half obvious, half offensive because of its obviousness. "I'm not deaf."

"Then you heard me?"

"What am I supposed to say that I haven't said already?"

"You're answer, for starters."

"My answer to what?"

"I can't believe…your answer to the question I asked you yesterday about getting married."

Luce leaned over slightly and looked at me, a wry smile pulled at one corner of her mouth. "Sometimes, Reeky, you sound like a fool. How many times do I have to answer you? If I didn't know you so well, I would have thought you were tap dancing around something." She glanced at the ceiling as if she was communing with an invisible spirit. "Naturally…oh, my goodness, look at the time." She patted me on my hand and immediately stood up. "Why didn't you tell me? I have to get up early tomorrow."

"Please don't go without telling me."

She shook her head, smiled, and chuckled softly. "It's the same as last time. Unlike you, I'm not in the habit of changing my mind. I need to talk to my sister tomorrow." This time she smiled more broadly while she looked at me.

So, I finally had my answer or answers. She had indeed heard me, and what was almost unbelievable, she said yes, or at least for Luce it was yes. I wanted to kiss her, but she was out of reach and heading toward the door before I could get up. "Wait," I said, trying to stop her. "What about your sister?"

Standing in the doorway, one foot already in the hall, Luce looked at me as if she were trying to recall something very important. "I'm moving in with her tomorrow." She started to move and then stopped. "Oh, I forgot, Reeky, dear." She rushed toward me as if she were going to fall into my arms but veered off at the last second, picked up her shoes and slipped them on, and then left without another word.

Chapter 20

That evening was one of the happiest in my life. Luce had given me her answer, and it was a resounding yes. We were going to be married, although how and when and all the rest of it had yet to be decided – had yet to be contemplated. But it didn't matter – nothing mattered – because she had accepted and some day she and I would be Mr. and Mrs. I couldn't help imagining that day, standing before a large, open field and facing a crowd of guests, while Luce in her white dress and veil is standing next to me. Turning toward her, I lift her veil and, as the guests cheer and clap, I lean over and gingerly, passionately, kiss her moist, red lips. I observe her smile and suddenly the music overwhelms us and we whisk or are whisked down the makeshift aisle to a specially constructed pavilion where our friends quickly assemble and congratulate us, slapping me on the back, kissing her on the cheek, and laughing and shouting at whatever people laugh and shout at during these events. I went over the dream details several times, altering the venue and the reception to increase the excitement I felt. In the end, at a climax of sorts, I think I settled on a cathedral and a formal wedding, with tuxedoes and white dresses, none of which were whiter than my beloved's.

I could have spent the entire night developing and redeveloping these images, but my eyes began to get heavy and soon my thoughts refused to follow any coherent order (I vaguely recall Luce standing next to me and wearing a bowler and a fake mustache) and before I knew it, I succumbed to a deep, restful sleep. Like always, I may or may not have dreamed, but the next thing that forced its way into my consciousness was the blaring sound of a crying baby, which immediately ceased when I grabbed its plastic neck and dropped it to the floor, where the back fell off the and the batteries rolled under the bed. I immediately sat up, groggily aware of what had just happened, and for a few seconds tried to understand if there was any substance to my nocturnal images, which were quickly dissolving. Finally coming to my senses, I shook my head and stretched my toes, and immediately forgot whatever I might have been dreaming. On my way to the bathroom, I noticed a poker chip on my dresser, a memento from our excursion to Lake Tahoe, and it was then that I recalled some bits and pieces about the ceremony.

I was suddenly filled with the warmth that came from the realization that I was going to be Luce's husband and that she and I were destined to live a magical life together. But as I stood somewhat groggily over the bowl, I started to wonder if this new status was merely a figment of my imagination. Did I really ask her to marry me? It took a few seconds, but that very moment came back to me with crystal clarity. But having metaphorically held my hand out to her, had she actually taken it and replied affirmatively? It seemed so yesterday, but the certainty of the night was quickly flushed away when I couldn't recall her exact response. Did she indicate a yes or a no? What did she say in response to my question, which I apparently phrased and rephrased I don't know how many times to get a straight answer. I might have put the entire blame on the TV and all the other distractions in my apartment, but I knew Luce well enough to understand that she didn't always respond with any geometric linearity. Naturally, things might have been a little easier had I been able to read most of her expressions, which she often wore on her sleeve – did a sneer in this case correspond to a 'yes,' was the dismissive wave of her right hand mean 'no,' and how was I to interpret a smile, particularly a condescending one? – and yet when I tried to make sense of these nonverbal expressions as a whole, I was at a loss as to what it could mean.

To suppress such doubts, I took a shower and thoughtfully dressed, donning my gray, pinstriped suit and a yellow, power tie. When everything was just about right (I straightened my shoulders a couple of times in the mirror), I noticed that I hadn't shaved. I took a dry razor and quickly scrapped my cheeks, neck, and chin, but when it was time to finish the job, I hesitated because I noticed the beginnings of a fine mustache sprouting beneath my nose. Since it complemented my suit and gave my face a strong, masculine edge, I decided to keep it for a while – unless Luce didn't approve. But when I returned to her response (I couldn't keep away from it), I was even less certain than before. Did she really say yes, or did I misread the signs? And what exactly did she mean when she said that she needed to talk to her sister? I didn't know the woman, although judging from a picture that Luce had, she resembled her sister in a vague, sinister way. Did Luce tell her sister everything? Did she seek her guidance? Did she mentally torture the poor girl? I had no way of knowing, just as I had no way of knowing anything else, except that I couldn't again demand an answer from Luce, not unless I wanted her to rethink her decision, if indeed it had been affirmative. Once outside, I sniffed the cool morning city air but practically gagged, because it smelled like garbage cans and human refuse.

I walked several blocks to the trolley stop. Grabbing the side of the first one that rounded the corner, I jumped on the running board, paid the conductor, and rode the noisy, clanging, rickety car down the hill to Market Street. I hiked a few more blocks to my office building, rode the elevator to the tenth floor, and opened the company's glass doors. I was immediately greeted by the rosy smile of the receptionist, who said that so-and-so was looking for me. Nodding affirmatively but not really paying attention to her, I strode quickly down the main hallway, sidestepping several employees hauling out paper-filled boxes from one of the offices, and finally arrived at my cubicle, where I plopped down into my chair. Instead of launching into accounts whose due dates were poised above my neck, I put my elbows on my desk and rested my forehead on my fists.

I couldn't understand it. I couldn't understand why it was so difficult to get out of her the simplest and most direct answer known to humankind – yes or no, I will or I won't, thumbs up or thumbs down, off with his head. Was it me, was I unique in this respect, or did others have the same problems? It didn't seem likely that others faced the same issue, since people around the world were getting married and divorced every minute of every day, and yet I wasn't willing to blame Luce, not just yet, because I loved her and I desperately wanted to be her husband.

But unlike last night, I couldn't come up with any wedding scenarios this morning, only images in which she was rolling on the ground, laughing because I assumed we were going to get married.

"And what exactly did I say, you numbskull?" I could see her demanding. "And on the basis of nothing you assumed that I would marry you instead of your handsome colleague in Seattle, who by the way has a manlier mustache?"

I shook the bad thoughts from my mind. I needed to get some clarity, and for some reason I thought that if I spoke to her now, I might finally get the straightforward answer that I had been seeking. But when I reached for the phone, the office manager's assistant, a slim, young woman whose sterile business clothes matched her expressionless face, placed a folder stuffed with papers on my desk directly in front of me.

"Mr. Rogers," she began, referring to our supervisor, the office manager. "Mr. Rogers says to redo the figures on Schedules A-F and make the other changes marked on Schedules G-J."

I nodded silently.

"Mr. Rogers needs the changes by COB today. COB means close of business."

I nodded again and scooted my chair up to my desk as a cue for her to leave.

"Mr. Rogers isn't pleased with mistakes, and he is even less happy the account is now late. Mr. Rogers wants more care taken with the accounts which you are responsible for. Two additional ones are due in three days."

Since I wasn't in the mood to hear about Mr. Rogers' likes and dislikes, I turned my back to the assistant and began dialing Luce's number. Mr. Rogers' mouthpiece didn't budge and continued relaying the other issues that Mr. Rogers had with my work. By the time she finally stomped off (doubtless, I was certain, to confer with Mr. Rogers about my attitude), Luce's phone was ringing.

The phone rang several times before a recorded message kindly informed me that the number I dialed had been disconnected. Certain that I had misdialed the number (possibly 5 instead of 6, 3 instead of 7, and something else instead of whatever), I reentered it and waited. There was a pause, and then the number started ringing – once, twice, again and again until the same less-than-pleasant recorded voice, which seemed intent on mocking me, stated again that the number had been disconnected, you fool. Disconnected? Was this my answer? After all that we had been through, after all the love and warmth, after everything that I had bloody-well tolerated, it had come down to this? I dialed the number six or seven more times, and each time I was confronted with the same insulting response. Fool, fool, fool! The final time was too much, and I slammed the phone down to let the recording and everyone else know that I wasn't happy.

"Mr. Rogers," my nemesis noted seemingly out of the blue (for some reason, she continued to hover nearby), "isn't going to be pleased if one of the company's phones…"

Before she had a chance to finish, I jumped up and stormed down the hall and out the front door. She followed me most of the way down the hall, never once letting up on what did and didn't please Mr. Rogers, reminding me once again as if I hadn't heard the first time that the changes were due C…O…B. "Mr. Rogers needs…," she was saying as I left the office, and I was certain that she would still be uttering the same thing until I returned.

I was only a few blocks from Luce's apartment when I remembered that she was leaving her apartment today and moving in with her sister. I had just finished struggling into the last parking space available when I recalled her words, which were suddenly clearer to me than anything else she said last night, and I couldn't help laughing over my forgetfulness and stupidity. Of course, her phone was disconnected, and since she wasn't moving into her own place, she wouldn't have a new number any time soon (her cell phone had mysteriously disappeared some time ago). Yes, I laughed, and loudly, because it relieved at least some of my anxiety, even if it didn't give me the answer that I needed. But instead of heading back to the office where I could learn more about Mr. Rogers and his needs, I decided to continue to her apartment anyway to catch her while the movers were doing their work.

When I arrived, I was surprised to find the front door locked (evidently, the movers hadn't propped it open while they worked) and, as I waited for something or someone (the movers or Luce herself), nothing at all happened – no one showed up. I stood directly in front of the building for at least thirty minutes waiting for someone to arrive. When I finally had it with waiting, I rang several of the buzzers to see if anyone knew what was happening. No one answered. It was as if the building were deserted, although I could still see her curtains on the inside of the living room window.

I returned to the office disappointed and dejected. Not only had I failed to reach her before the move, but I didn't have any way of contacting her, since I didn't know where her sister lived. On top of that, five minutes later I was treated to another lecture about Mr. Rogers, this time about what the great man expected from his employees.

It was nearly midnight when I finally got home from work. I checked my messages (there weren't any) and then flopped onto the couch. I wanted to sleep, but I was too tired and my nerves too strained to allow my eyes to close blissfully. Furthermore, I was afraid of falling asleep – I was afraid of missing Luce's call should she actually try to reach me at this late hour. Will she call, I asked myself, and why didn't she leave a message, I demanded as if she were close enough to hear? After a few minutes, however, the idea that she wouldn't call ceased to be as distressing as it had been earlier in the day. Maybe I was too tired to care, maybe I had expended my emotional energies fretting about things during the day, maybe whatever it was I was finally ready to accept the idea that she wasn't going to call this evening. To calm my nerves while I waited for her call (just in case she called), I turned on the TV and watched a baseball game that was first aired over twenty years ago. Since I completed my work, I had the luxury of staying up as late as I wanted even if Mr. Rogers didn't approve.

An hour later, I was awoken by the soft rumble of my phone. It was a text message from Luce. Without so much as a 'Dear Reeky,' she provided her sister's address (not the phone number) and noted that she (Luce) would be out of town for a couple of weeks – in Seattle, of all places – and that she would "contact" (the pronoun was missing) when she returned. She added a P.S. (without having appended her name) to the effect that I should not under any circumstances try to get in touch with her during this time (the "NOT" was in capitals as if the word needed such emphasis to get through to me). That was it. There wasn't anything more substantive or concrete to the note. Obviously, it was a little puzzling. Why would she go out of town for a couple of weeks without telling me beforehand, and why would her destination have to be Seattle, the home of…? But since it was something that she addressed to me, I was determined to fulfill her wishes to the letter. After all, she was writing to me, which suggested that all was not lost and that I still had some reason to hope regarding my proposal (why else would she have sent the note?).

One evening a few days before Luce was due to return, I decided to drive by her sister's house to make sure I could find it when the time came.

It was a small bungalow in one of the nicer sections of Hayward. The street lights had just flickered on, and I parked across the street in the shadows between the lights, keeping the engine idling because I wasn't planning to stay long. I also wasn't getting out of the car. The only thing I wanted to do, while I was seated low behind the wheel and staring at the glowing windows of the house, was to imagine Luce shuffling through the rooms in her pink, oversized, fluffy slippers. Having accomplished that, I was about to ease the car away when I noticed Luce walk into the living room and stand in front of the large window that looked out onto the front yard. Dressed casually, she seemed more beautiful than ever, her face and body practically glowing in the yellow light of the room. For a few seconds, I thought she might be alone, but then another woman came in and stood beside her and, whispering something in her ear, led her away from the widow and apparently out of the room. The other woman could have been Luce's sister (she looked vaguely like Luce), and after they disappeared I thanked my stars that there wasn't a man in sight, especially my mustached former colleague. Once again, I was ready to leave, but this time I hesitated because Luce reappeared in the window without the other woman. Cupping her hands against the glass and placing her forehead against her hands, she stared into the darkness toward my car. Without waiting to see if she recognized me or my car, I sped off with a slight screech of the back tires.

Chapter 21

I made a more formal visit to the house the following weekend. Although Luce's note was ambiguous (the missing pronoun), I pretended that it was absolutely clear and that Luce would be waiting for me at her sister's place at the end of two weeks.

It was midmorning on a bright, cloudless day (cloudless, that is, outside of San Francisco), and as I pulled up in front of the house exactly where I parked previously, I half-expected to see Luce puttering around the house, maybe doing some gardening or repairing this or that for her sister. I wasn't troubled in the least when I didn't immediately spot her. If by chance she wasn't there (maybe she was running an errand and hadn't anticipated the time of my visit), I was prepared to wait, chatting pleasantly with her sister, until she returned. And, yes, the possibility of marriage was still very much on my mind, if only because Luce had given me information about her whereabouts – and what was the point in that if she wasn't entertaining the idea?

I rang the doorbell twice in succession, and one more time to be sure when the first two rings weren't answered. I was about to ring a fourth time, if need be pushing the button harder and longer, when a young woman opened the door about six inches and peered at me through the crack. Her reluctance to open the door fully, and the manner in which she eyed me through the crack, made me wonder if she were afraid of something outside or hesitant to let me see inside. For a moment, though, I saw all I needed to see. I recognized those steel-blue eyes, the elegant nose, the blood-red lips, and the straight blond hair – I knew at once and without doubt that it was Madeline, her sister, the very woman I had seen in the window with Luce.

Madeline was a mystery. Everything that I knew about her came from her sister. Luce, though, was generally tightlipped about the younger woman (by two-and-a-half years), offering preciously little save that the two were as different as night and day and that Madeline had a dark side. According to Luce, there had never been any question as to their relationship, although sometimes she found it hard to believe that they had grown up in the same house. "We're sisters, I suppose," Luce once said, "but we're practically strangers." When pressed to elaborate, she called me an idiot and accused me of being more interested in phantasms than in real people. But I suspect that Luce's reticence was a reaction to leaving a nice apartment in a great location in San Francisco to go live with the younger woman in her house (Madeline owned her house). Then again, maybe Luce was simply being Luce. Whatever the reason, when I came face to face with Madeline – who, by the way, was every bit as attractive as her older sister – I didn't know what to say and for a few moments stared, probably open jawed, hoping that she would tell me why I was there. I came to my senses when she refused to open the door, forcing us to converse through the small aperture between the door and the doorjamb.

"So, it's you," Madeline said. The deadpan sound of her voice was familiar.

"Madeline? Is that you?" Smiling pleasantly, I gave her my name. "Well, it's nice to meet you. Luce told me so much…"

Without replying or even looking away, she began to close the door, which I halted with the toe of my left shoe.

"Wait, wait. Where's Luce? Didn't she tell you I was coming by?"

"In a manner of speaking," she replied, releasing the pressure on the door though not opening it up.

"What did she say? May I see her?" At this point, I could sense one of Luce's terrible games taking shape. But what I found out practically floored me.

"Not right now."

"Why," I persisted.

"Because, smarty pants, she's dead."

"What? That's not funny. May I see her?"

"No joke, Jack. Luce killed herself a couple days ago. But I suppose you didn't know."

"No," I gasped, "what are you talking about. Luce isn't dead. Luce [I stated her last name], your sister, right?"

"Right as rain, but dead as a duck."

I suddenly felt sick, and my head began to throb angrily. It can't be true, I told myself, because I loved Luce and we were going to be married (I hoped). She wouldn't have killed herself without first giving me her answer to my proposal.

"No," I muttered feebly. Tiny stars began dancing before my eyes, and for a few seconds I was certain that I was going to faint.

"Yes. She hung herself from the clothes bar in the hall closet. She created a noose from a man's tie. One of yours, I presume. Of course, it could have been anybody's. I found her as I was about to hang up my coat. I wanted to puke. Have you ever seen what happens to…"

"Anybody's? Who else could it…no."

"Yes."

"No, I don't believe it. It can't be true. It can't. No, prove it." I gathered my strength and, looking straight at her (or what I could see of her), demanded proof of something I refused to believe.

"Prove what? That ties can kill or that this particular tie could be anybody's?"

"No, no, I mean, show me something that proves she's dead. Jokes like these aren't funny. They hurt people."

"Jokes?"

"Why didn't you call me? If there was truly…"

"Why didn't I call you? Why would anyone call you, since you were the cause of it? The note…"

"Note? What note? Did she leave a note? Let me see it."

Madeline managed to push my toe aside and, without another word, closed the door. I didn't resist; I didn't have the strength. But just as I was about to turn and go (what else could I do?), she returned with a ragged piece of notebook paper that she slipped between the door and the doorjamb. Keeping the door nearly closed, she said, "Here, hot snot, read it for yourself."

It was a sheet of yellow, legal-size notebook paper that had been crumpled and then meticulously opened and smoothed out. My hands were shaking as I grasped its edges and recognized my beloved's familiar crude scrawl across the surface in blood-red ink:

Dear M, I'm sorry, time is short. [Something illegible here] is waiting. There are many things I should have said. Maybe [something else illegible]. After I'm gone, R will come by. He always does. Please tell him something. You're good at that. XXX [again, illegible],

    L

I was dumbfounded. I turned to Madeline, who had opened the door wide enough to expose her face (and I hate to admit it, but at that moment I couldn't help admiring her smooth, marble-perfect features and her dark eyes, which left me helpless in a way that Luce's eyes could never do. In fact, she was even more beautiful than my former beloved and, for some reason, I didn't feel the least bit guilty admitting it), and I demanded to know what the paper in my hands actually meant.

"This doesn't make sense. This isn't a suicide note. It's a…I don't know what it is, but I'll be damned if it has anything to do with death. She's running an errand or something."

"I hope you are damned for what you did. It's all she left. By the way, I thought you were taller. Anyway, if you don't believe it, take it up with her in the afterlife, if by some miracle you reach the same place." She hesitated as if she were trying to stifle a sob. "In fact, why don't you contact the police if you don't think the note's real. Better yet, check out the morgue if you don't believe it. She's still there. Go ahead, buckshot. And while you're at it, why don't you ask yourself why she did it. I know why she did it. This paper speaks for itself." Madeline ripped the note from my hand and, waving it back in front of my face, she practically screamed that I had driven Luce to take such drastic means to fix her life – I had driven her, she sputtered, to the point of desperation and beyond. Calming down a little, she added, "My sister never had a good word to say about you, and I can see why."

The door was now entirely open, and I could see Madeline from top to bottom. She was wearing a form-fitting white blouse and skin-tight jeans, and her shimmering hair flowed freely over her shoulders and around her perfect face. Once again, she was beautiful, and for an instant I couldn't tell whether it was her beauty or Luce's apparent demise that made me weak in the knees. Nevertheless, the fact that she was blaming me for something that I still couldn't entirely accept, something that if it were true I couldn't have been responsible for, sickened me and, losing control, I hollered for Luce to come to the door.

"Luce, Luce," I shouted, "Luce, where are you? It's me, Luce!" If my knees weren't weak, if I still retained the necessary physical strength, I would have pushed Madeline aside (gently, of course, one doesn't manhandle a fine work of art) and investigated each room in the small house until I either found her or uncovered evidence that she was alive or dead.

Madeline didn't seem surprised by my behavior. It was as if she had expected it, as if she knew ahead of time that I would react in this way. And her immobility in response to my violence also suggested that she wasn't in the least troubled or fearful that my behavior would devolve into something worse, something possibly directed against her. Indeed, while I was yelling, she folded her arms across her ample chest, leaned against the doorjamb, and crossed her legs, an attitude which clearly suggested that she was enjoying the show and that she wouldn't have to move to let an angry bull charge into the house. After I had obviously yelled for the last time, she smiled a bitter but beautiful smile and calmly uttered, "Satisfied?"

I stared blankly for a few moments until Madeline unexpectedly said something about my moustache. "I love it. I really do. It makes you look…"

I didn't hear the rest. Madeline didn't move as I staggered away from the door, plodding down the long sidewalk in front of the house and across the street to where my car, a pathetic, beat-up piece of junk I had once been proud to own, was parked. I had to fumble with the keys for a few minutes before the door would yield (my eyes were filled with tears, making it hard to see where and how the key fit) and, once behind the wheel, I paused again to shed a few tears into my lap. I sped off without locking the seatbelt. Glancing over my left shoulder, I noticed that Madeline was still where I left her, a Grecian statue with the ghost of a smile that no one but da Vinci could have replicated.

Chapter 22

I got lost leaving the neighborhood (I should have turned right instead of left, and I missed an intersection because I had difficulty seeing through my tears), but as soon as I got my bearings, I headed back to the city, back to a place where I could remember Luce properly – her dark eyes and almost translucent cheeks, her golden hair shimmering and dancing in the cool breezes off the Pacific Ocean, and the incredible life we could have had once we were married. As her husband, I could have helped her find a way out of whatever was oppressing her. But what was it? What drove her to the edge of the precipice and beyond? And despite Madeline's coarse accusation, I was positive that I didn't bear any responsibility for Luce's problems or her resultant demise.

We are all responsible for our own lives, but Luce never once suggested that I was making her life unendurable or that she was contemplating something extreme with her life. I can say this without doubt, because she wasn't someone who shied away from expressing her feelings, even if her words were cruel and damaging. If I had done half of what Madeline suggested, Luce would have laid into me without the least compunction, calling me a fool, liar, idiot, or whatever else she found suitable at the moment. She also wasn't the kind of person to keep troubling things bottled-up inside, especially not while the cause of these troubling things walked the earth in blissful ignorance. Remember her run-in with the truck and trailer? I know without a doubt that she would have torn into him physically and verbally despite the twin facts that she wasn't hurt and that many positive things came from the incident. Luce wasn't a delicate flower, and if you yanked off one petal, she would have come after you with the other ninety-nine, in addition to all the thorns she possessed. Given all this, how could I (or anyone else, for that matter) have led her down the narrow path to oblivion? No, not me, and it wasn't anything that I could have done. I knew Luce loved me, and therefore I couldn't understand why she would have taken her own life.

While waiting at a red light before turning onto the highway toward San Francisco, I glanced absently out the windshield, observing all the silent, faceless buildings surrounding me, wondering which one of them might be able to answer the horrible question of why. Why did she do it? Just as the light turned green, I noticed a particularly nondescript building on the other side of the street. I don't know what drew me to the place, especially as the driver behind me was testing the limits of his car's horn, but I immediately pulled out of the lane, drove to the other side of the road, turned right, and angled the nose of the car toward what I thought might be the entrance of the building's parking lot. While I waited for the cross traffic to thin so I could enter, I spotted a sign next to the building which announced in warm, soft letters the cold, hard fact that the building was the county morgue.

Staring at the building as if I had the power to penetrate its thick walls, I tried to imagine what it was like on the inside. I could easily imagine sterile white rooms that reeked of embalming fluid and putrefying flesh, and I noticed long, empty corridors that creaked and groaned but led nowhere and connected nothing. What were the workers like? Were they soulless automatons who felt nothing in the presence of dead bodies? Did they go home each night reeking of death and yet eating and sleeping as if it were only a matter of business? As I recreated more and more details, I began to see Luce in one of those white rooms, lying naked on a cold, metal tray, her dignity covered only by a thin, white cloth that began at the top of her head and ended at her ankles, her pale white feet and red toenails callously exposed. No, I told myself, as I finally had an opening to cross the lane and enter the parking lot – no, it's not like that at all. Luce isn't dead, and she isn't being housed like a dead fish in a place like that, with all the other pathetic, filthy individuals who didn't have the decency to die in a hospital like everyone else.

"No," I said out loud as I put the car into motion and headed across the street, "Luce isn't dead, and I'm going to prove it."

The parking lot was practically deserted as I headed toward the main doors. I drove the car into a space only a few yards away and then stopped and, for a few minutes, stared blankly at the imposing edifice. Observing the glistening glass doors, each of which was at least ten feet high and seven to eight feet wide, I mentally measured the distance from the car to the doors, not excluding the step that raised the doors another six inches or so from the sidewalk, and then calculated the time it would take to get from the car to the doors, and then from the doors to the lobby inside. Once inside, assuming the doors were unlocked, I would locate the concierge to find out where the bodies are kept, and once there begin the arduous task of sorting through each one until I located Luce (and, for some reason, I assumed that this was the normal process for locating a loved one). But before I shut off the engine and made my way toward the doors, I began to wonder how many bodies I would have to sort through to find Luce – there could be a lot of them, I reasoned, and it could be midnight before I finished the dull and disheartening work. Wouldn't it therefore be better, I asked myself, if I got a bite to eat before I began handling all the corpses? I couldn't help thinking that the smell of the chemicals mixed with the odor of decaying flesh could rob me of my appetite and hence compromise my ability to complete what was now beginning to seem a long and arduous task. Smiling at my stupidity, I rested my forehead on the steering wheel and began to cry.

I don't know how or why I conjured up such strange images, but about five minutes later after I was done crying, I knew that I couldn't go in there under any circumstances. It was foolish to doubt Madeline – nobody in their right mind would make up something that could be disproved so easily – and it didn't matter whether or not I believed her, because it was obvious that Luce was dead, and there was nothing that I could do to change this mundane fact. Furthermore, as much as I would have wanted to pay my last respects to her, I knew that I couldn't do it this way. I couldn't stand seeing her lying on an oversized cookie sheet, the color drained from her flesh. I couldn't bear looking at her motionless, gelatinous eyes peering blindly into nothingness for all eternity. And I couldn't tolerate the marks of her demise across her once beautiful neck. As much as I wanted to see her one more time, I refused to see her in a way that would make an indelible blot on her memory, which I wanted to be filled with images that I knew she would appreciate, images of Luce as she was in life.

I turned the car around and headed to San Francisco.

Chapter 23

It was a miracle that I made it home in one piece, because I don't recall a single thing about the drive. Given my emotions, it's not surprising that my mind wasn't completely focused on driving, but I can't imagine how I managed to negotiate the city traffic, the crisscross bustle of cars, the hubbub of pedestrians, and the narrow, one-way streets without a single mishap. Perhaps there is something to luck, although I didn't feel lucky when I finally came to my senses and struggled with the lock to my door, which seemed oddly heavy as I pushed it open.

Even though the day was still relatively young, my apartment was dark and strangely cold, making me think that it was not dissimilar to the place where Luce was now resting. I dropped onto the couch, to the exact spot where I imagined Luce preferred to sit, and stayed there for a couple hours or so, staring blankly into the space in front of me. I might have remained in a vegetative state for some time had it not occurred to me that Luce would be given a funeral at some point. Even the monstrous but beautiful Madeline wouldn't deny her sister that much, and I was suddenly determined to attend the event either to pay my respects or, hopefully, to see Luce appear from behind a curtain to disprove Madeline's horrible story. I could feel a smile creasing my cheeks, and for a few moments I was practically chuckling because I would have my beloved back and, at the same time, be able to put Madeline in her place. But after a while, it occurred to me that I might not be invited to the event. You can never tell what some people will do, especially if they're out to make your life unpleasant.

Pulling my phone out of my pocket, I searched for recent callers and dialed the one number I didn't recognize. I wasn't eager to speak to Madeline, but I was determined to get all the information I could about the funeral, if she was going to hold one.

"Look," I insisted, when she hesitated to provide the details, "I only want to pay my respects. I'm not going to cause trouble, and…and…can't you see that I loved her and wouldn't have done anything to cause her to…" I couldn't say the words. "Please, don't hang up. I know you're going to announce the funeral in the paper, and I can get the time and location there. I'd prefer to keep this on a friendly basis. Luce told me many times how much she loved and admired you. Please, don't shut me out."

There was a long pause while I waited breathlessly for her decision. After a hush-like sound and several vague scraping noises, Madeline came back on the line. Expecting the worst, I heard her sniff two or three times as if to suggest that she wasn't really interested in what I had to say, after which she coughed delicately and in a nonchalant tone asked me what Luce said about her. If I hadn't been so fearful of upsetting her, I would have laughed out loud at her cold, selfishness in the face of her sister's death. Luce was barely cold, and Madeline wanted to know what her sister said about her. Well, I gave her a few trite statements (I wasn't in a state to come up with anything more interesting than Luce liked her sense of humor, Luce was jealous of her beauty, Luce admired her unerring fashion sense, and a few other chestnuts), and to my surprise they not only satisfied her, they encouraged her to ask for more details.

"I thought she hated that blouse," Madeline said at one point. There was a pause as if she were trying to remember exactly what Luce had said.

"No, no, no," I insisted, "she loved it. She couldn't tell you the truth because…because she was jealous of you."

"Are you sure?"

"Yes, absolutely positive."

"I have to say that she did dress atrociously at times, no matter how much I tried to help."

The flattery worked. Madeline stated in the same flat tone that Luce often used that there wasn't going to be a funeral. "She's going to be cremated, and I suppose I'll dump her ashes somewhere. I think she wanted it, although it sounds a little creepy to me. But if you must know, I'm going to have a small gathering Saturday to remember her and all that. I suppose you can come," she said and paused for a couple of moments. I don't know why, but the mention of a small gathering – did she say intimate? – reminded me of the small gathering where I first met Luce. Madeline seemed ready to say something else, but she hung up without another word. Despite her tone, I knew that she was eager to see me, but only if I had something to add about Luce's admiration of her.

Chapter 24

I didn't go to work that week. I was in a terrible state, and I wasn't interested in what Mr. Rogers felt or what our clients were demanding. Even if I were somehow able to find my way to the office, I couldn't have fudged a single number for anyone, much less engaged in the long, tiresome conversations about absolutely nothing that were expected of individuals in my position. I realize that everyone loses someone sooner or later and that most people return to their normal lives if for no other reason than to cope with their loss. But my situation was different. I loved Luce with a passion and intensity that went beyond the pedestrian feelings most people have for their loved ones. No, that's not right. It wasn't simply that I loved her. Most people love somebody. It was the case that my feelings for her were of such depth that it was impossible for me to contemplate her as someone that I once loved. She was an integral part of me: She was essential to my being, to my very existence, and it would have been easier to lose an arm or a leg than to lose her. She was my heart and soul. There was no me without her. She was me, and there could be no life if she were dead. There were a few brief moments when I accepted Luce's demise and, after carefully weighing my ability to continue on without her, decided that I too would do away with myself (pirouetting off Golden Gate Bridge, for example, or placing my mouth over my car's exhaust pipe), but what saved me from taking such an irrevocable step were the memories – the last living artifacts of Luce's existence – and the fact that I simply lacked the energy to undertake something so rigorous (the body always struggles to retain life).

So, how does one get through each day after something like this happens (and very early on I ceased doubting the fact of Luce's non-existence)? Do you gather up everything that was once hers – the comb, the stray hairs, the sweater, and the last unwashed dish she used for dinner – and place them all in a special place where you could look at them, touch them, use them to convince yourself that she is still with you in some sense? Do you talk to people who knew her, perhaps going out of your way to connect with those who could tell you something about her that would enhance your own memories (and does it matter if their memories aren't true in every respect as long as they're consonant with your own conception of her)? Do you go out with friends to distract yourself and end up mooning over all the great times you had together visiting this and watching that? Do you call on God, ask forgiveness, demand that He take your life instead, and pray that when your time comes – and pray that it comes soon – you'll be reunited with the one person who made your life whole? Or do you sometimes pretend that she isn't really dead but outside somewhere waiting for you, and so you go outside and walk through the streets quietly calling her name? When this doesn't work, do you go to her old apartment, ring the bell so many times that a light comes on her window (making you momentarily think that it was all a bad joke and that at any second she's going to open the door) and someone finally comes to the door? A short, plain-looking young woman who could stand to lose some weight explains several times that she is now the occupant of that ethereal place and that she didn't know Luce. She refuses your request to come inside and then threatens to call the police if you don't immediately leave. What do you do then?

I went home and began a conversation with Luce. I spoke to her as if she were inside of me, and I explained everything that had happened, how I met with Madeline and then all the rest of it, including the poor girl who now occupied her apartment. The latter incident was hilarious, because I told her that the unfortunate young woman probably thought I was a madman searching for a ghost. If she actually called the police, I would have given almost anything to be a fly on the wall to hear her explain how a tall, rather good-looking stranger with a masculine mustache came to the door and demanded the presence of someone who, he claimed, was dead, as if she naturally kept dead bodies on the premises. To top it off, this stranger, who to all outward appearances seemed perfectly normal, left in a huff when she didn't produce the body and disappeared in the night calling out the dead person's name, which I vaguely recall doing.

"I know you're gone," I said in the darkness of my apartment, "But I also know you're still with me and wouldn't leave me. I feel it as much as I feel anything else. You didn't leave me, Luce, and I know you're going to be closer to me than ever before."

I perked up a little by the end of the week, although there were still many times when I broke down and was only a step or two from diving out the window or hurling myself in front of a passing bus. But apart from these moments, I was getter better and increasingly interested in seeing Madeline to relive the past.

"I'm only doing it for you, my love, only for you," I told Luce. "And I promise you I won't pretend you're gone and never coming back. I won't pretend we can't be with each other, feeling and experiencing the same things we always did. Nothing between us will ever change."

I hesitated just before locking the door behind me. "When we get back, Luce, you and I are going to go to some beautiful place, maybe Carmel, and we're going to have the wedding as if nothing happened. We can make it simple. Maybe we can do it some evening at the edge of the water, while the moon breaks up on its surface. We'll finally do it, and then live the way we should have lived from the beginning."

Chapter 25

It was a blazing day, especially for San Francisco, and I had to shield my eyes as I drove to Hayward. At the last moment, I was reluctant to leave my apartment – immediately correcting myself by noting that it was "our" apartment – because I inexplicably felt that I was also leaving her, leaving the place where she cozied up at the corner of the couch or stretched out on the bed. But I resolved the conundrum by bringing her with me, and I let her know that know that I wasn't planning to stay long and that we could leave any time she felt uncomfortable being there. "Maybe when we get back, we can…," I began but couldn't finish. I was now within sight of Madeline's house.

I had expected to see a lot of activity on the street and around the house, people bustling about and exchanging stories about Luce and her life. But nothing appeared out of the ordinary. If anything, the area seemed deserted, practically devoid of life. The house itself seemed dark, but this was probably only an illusion caused by the bright sun (which was much brighter in Hayward than in the city) and cool interior visible through the screen door. Perhaps I was early, maybe I was late, but regardless I was there and determined to make the best of it.

I got out of my car and walked up the walkway. For a few moments I half expected Luce to show up, perhaps walking toward the house carrying a bag of groceries or maybe stepping out from behind a bush to greet me or possibly doing some repairs on the house. Unlike the last time I was here, the place looked rundown and decaying (the front lawn was brown and dying, and there were cobwebs on the outside corners of the living room window), as if Luce's absence had taken the life out of it, too. Everything was quiet, as I noted, and instead of ringing the bell, I walked in (surely, the door was left open for this specific purpose) and looked around.

I was a little surprised that nothing seemed to have been prepared either for the event or for the occupants who lived here. I glanced into the kitchen, and everything there was neat and tidy, and so I couldn't help wondering if I had the wrong house or the wrong day. I started to back out to make sure I was at the right place when I noticed the back door, which was on the other side of the kitchen and wide open. The screen door was closed, but I could see something outside – a bare, feminine leg – in the back yard when I angled my head to the side. Forgetting the possibility that I might be considered an intruder, I walked over to the door expecting to find Madeline outside, relaxing in the sun. When I got within a foot of the door, I could clearly see the top of a small, feminine straw hat keeping the sun out of the wearer's eyes, while the rest of the individual was relaxing in a lounger, sipping a drink from a straw, and enjoying a magazine and the bright sun.

It was odd that Madeline would relax on a day like this, at a time when she should be up and honoring her sister's memory, but after mulling it over I couldn't get too upset. She looked comfortable and attractive, and she deserved a little downtime after everything that had happened. Inching closer, I could see from the side that she was wearing a skimpy bikini, hardly more than a few straps, and as I observed her more carefully (and I couldn't take my eyes off her, since the bikini was exactly like the one that Luce often wore), I was struck by how closely she resembled her sister, possibly a little more athletic, if you like that kind of thing.

Well, I wasn't going to spend the day watching Madeline tan, especially since I was planning to revisit Carmel with Luce's ghost. It was only out of courtesy that I decided to say hello and pay my respects or whatever you do when it's your beloved who's gone. However, I stopped before I pulled the screen door open, for I noticed that Madeline had a small mole on her right thigh in almost the exact spot that Luce did, and the sight of it brought back memories of Lake Tahoe and every other time that I had seen and kissed that lovely little blotch. But my reminiscences were unexpectedly cut short when Madeline sensed my presence and turned around. I yanked the door open, practically off its hinges, and charged outside, tripping over a leather camera case and landing on the seat of my pants.

Propping myself up with my arms, I stared at the woman I had taken for Madeline and gasped, "Luce?"

"Of course, you idiot. Who did you think it was?"

"I thought you were….you were…dead."

"What are you babbling about?

"The note, your sister said…."

"What note?"

"You said you were going away."

"I did, and now I'm back. Do you think you could get up? You look like a circus clown sitting like that."

I stood up and brushed myself off. "Your sister said you were, you were…gone forever."

"What? I went to Seattle."

"But she said you were…" I kept scanning her from head to toe, and every inch of her reassured me that she was not dead but positively alive.

"You're talking nonsense. Would you please get out of my sun?"

"She said you were dead. You killed yourself…" I couldn't finish, because she started laughing and dropped her cheap tabloid.

"Oh, my God," she sputtered and continued laughing. She placed her drink on the patio so that it wouldn't get spilled and stared at me. Noticing my bewildered expression, she broke into a wild guffaw. When she was at last calm, she said, "Maddie must have been playing a game. The joke's on you, you moron. Well, well, isn't she the one."

"My God, my God," was about all I could utter at the moment. I didn't know what to say. There wasn't anything to say. It was clear that I had been the dupe of a joke so monstrous that it lacked a parallel in civilized history. What made it even worse was that Luce started laughing again, making me feel that I had somehow deserved whatever I got.

When Luce's laughter seemed at last to have subsided, she slipped the tops of her sunglasses down her nose and squinted at me. "For God's sake, wash that ridiculous thing off your lip. How can I concentrate with that....but didn't you say you read my note?"

"Yes," I muttered.

"About leaving?"

"Yes."

"And from that you deduced that I was dead?"

"Yes...I mean, no. Madeline said it was a suicide note and that you had taken your life because of me."

Naturally, this sent Luce off into another peal of laughter. When she was calm again, she picked up her glass and leaned back into her chair. "In the first place, you dolt, I am very much alive, as you can see." She took a long drink before continuing. "And in the second, I wouldn't kill myself for anyone, especially not for some simpleton who falls for such pranks." She laughed a couple of times before she could finish. "Didn't you read the message I sent you? I went to Seattle to take care of few things and, on my way back, I considered your proposal." She chuckled slightly and took a drink to cover it up.

What may have been funny a few minutes earlier was now becoming decidedly tiresome. I was furious with Madeline, and I couldn't fathom why anyone could have done such a thing. And I was also getting tired of Luce, who not only found my predicament amusing but who still couldn't give me a simple answer to my proposal. Nevertheless, the fact that she had heard my proposal and, coupled with her trip to Seattle to wrap up some personal affairs (hopefully, dumping that ass of a former colleague), piqued my interest and momentarily stopped me from storming away.

"Of course, I remember," I responded while observing the delicate undulations of her smooth legs and the fulsome size of her breasts as they struggled to escape the thin cords of fabric that held them in place.

Luce smiled and picked up her magazine. Once more making herself comfortable in the lounger, she began thumbing through the pages, pausing now and then to study a particular picture or advertisement.

You know, I have to say that the situation was kind of amusing. Any other time I would have gone ballistic over her continued reticence regarding what only a few moments ago seemed like a matter of life and death. But as I watched her flip through that stupid magazine and then place the straw to her lips and practically kiss out the cool contents of her glass, while at the same time acknowledging my presence only if I blocked the sun, I suddenly didn't care – I didn't care what her answer was or if she finally broke up with my colleague, who unexpectedly seemed a little more sympathetic, for it was clear that he endured the same sorts of things that I experienced at Luce's delicate hands and carefully painted nails. Maybe that was why he was hoping to be "liberated" from something. Maybe that was why he had to go to Seattle. I was about to leave when Luce started rattling on about some reality-star's marriage or divorce (I don't recall which), peppering her monologue with her opinions on celebrity marriages, the difficulties of cohabitations, fine German cameras, the absurdity of certain mustaches, and all the rest. I listened to her for a couple of minutes (more out of amazement than interest), but then both she and her inane chatter began fading into nothingness when I heard a slight noise behind me.

The noise, a hollow, wood-like creak, emanated from the kitchen. I turned and caught sight of someone on the other side of the screen door. She (and I could tell it was a woman because of her slim, gently curved shape and the feminine movements of her neck and shoulders) stood a few feet back from the door, engulfed in shadows too deep for me to make out her facial features. For some reason, her presence seemed inexplicably odd and possibly a little disturbing. I don't know. I suppose I was startled to see someone else in the house, since the place seemed deserted earlier and Luce hadn't indicated that anyone else was around. Then again, since the woman went about her business without apparently being aware of my presence, I had the uncomfortable feeling that I was watching something that I shouldn't, that I was intruding on someone's privacy. But before I had a chance to turn away, the woman turned and looked directly at me, twisting her slight shoulders in a way which suggested that she hadn't noticed my presence earlier and was surprised to find me observing her. I think she must have smiled a few seconds later – the outline of one of her cheeks against a bright object in the room seemed to broaden – and she walked toward the screen door, slowly, as though she wasn't surprised at all, as though she recognized me and was pleased that I was there. Once at the door, she patted the dust from a small section of the screen and, clearly smiling, briefly pressed her face against the screen like a kitten playing a game with me, leaving behind traces of her red lipstick. She immediately receded back into the shadows when I took a half-step toward the door.

What was I to think? The woman behind the screen door was Madeline, who along with her sister was apparently relishing this appalling joke. My initial surprise at her unexpected appearance quickly morphed into anger, for what seemed so funny to her and her sister could have had disastrous consequences – but I already mentioned that. Luckily, I had only lost a week of my life mourning for someone I thought I loved, and I still had a job (the office left messages every day, each one expressing Mr. Roger's regrets over my loss and inquiring when I could come in to explain certain accounts). For these things and for everything else that welled up in my mind, I wanted to run after her, I wanted to crash through the screen to make a point, I wanted to take her by her pretty neck and…and…but I couldn't. It wasn't in me to do such things. Standing there, mulling over Madeline's cruel and humiliating behavior, observing her slim figure and the manner in which she was using it to draw me towards her, something else stirred inside me and I realized that for the first time in my life I was actually in love.

- - - -))) - -)) – ((- - (((- - - -